well deserved

michael loyd gray

SOL BOOKS PROSE SERIES

well deserved

michael loyd gray

SOL BOOKS

Minneapolis

Published by Sol Books,
an imprint of Skywater Publishing Company,
P.O. Box 24568, Minneapolis, MN 55424.
www.solbooks.com

Library of Congress Cataloging-in-Publication Data
Gray, Michael Loyd.
   Well Deserved: A Novel / by Michael Loyd Gray.
      p. cm. — (Sol Books Prose Series)
      ISBN 978-0-9793081-7-8 (pbk.)
      ISBN 978-0-9793081-9-2 (e-book)
      1. Nineteen seventies—Fiction. 2. Illinois—Social life and
customs—Fiction. 3. City and town life—Fiction. I. Title.
PS3607.R3957W45 2010
813'.6—dc22   2008032398

Summary
The folks of Argus, from the small-time dealer to the returning
Vietnam vet, the townie grocery clerk and the new sheriff, all
know what they want out of life, but the paths to their desires
are conflicted and unclear. In a narrative with all the clarity
and determination of a prophecy, *Well Deserved* chronicles the
struggles of these four people as they come to the stark realization
that their paths are not solitary, but entwined, and their very lives
hinge on one shared moment.

Photo Credits
Shutterstock, cover

This book is dedicated to Monique Raphel High,
who really did help me discover how to be a better writer;
and to my mother, Dorothy Gray,
who has believed in my wacky and disreputable desire
to write when others did not.

I want to also mention Stuart Dybek,
who has always been accessible when I wanted advice.

To Elizabeth George and the Elizabeth George Foundation,
I say thanks, again, for the writing grant so generously
awarded to me.

I also dedicate my work to the memory of Daniel Curley,
a good writer and a good teacher and the first real writer
to take an interest in my work.

Finally, to the 1960s and early 1970s,
when the music still lived.

"If you don't know where you're going,
any road will take you there."
— George Harrison

The Three Days

1970

1.

Jesse

In the early spring of that restless year, before the leaves had come back green and full on the trees, Jesse Archer could look out a window from his decaying trailer in the woods and see the causeway road across Lake Argus pointing at him like a dagger. Or perhaps like a sword. The long white road was very narrow and straight and stretched nearly a mile before it reached shore again, piercing the Y intersection tucked against Jesse's halcyon woods. Maples, sycamores, and walnuts were abundant and tall and would soon be thick again. New signs of growth were obvious every day. Jesse had felt quite naked and exposed there all winter, even when snow filled the gaps between the trees and accumulated on his roof, and he longed for the enveloping leafy camouflage to blossom and cloak him from sight.

The trailer was poorly insulated and a bitch in winter, which had been cold and snowy, and sometimes Jesse slept on the beer-stained couch inside a sleeping bag and under several thick quilts because the warmth from the trailer's heating strips was strongest there. But the wooden trailer was loosely-built and so quite airy in spring and summer when the canopy of trees protected it from the sun, and it was pleasant enough until the summer humidity set in; then Jesse sometimes slept naked on the couch with a small fan directed at him, or even outside on the ground where he could look up through a gap in the trees at the sparkling stars or the moon. He had moved into the trailer the year before, when a man first walked on the moon, and he had sat up much of that night smoking dope and checking the moon skeptically — trying to decide if it was really happening or just propaganda concocted from some Hollywood movie set.

The humidity was still a ways off and he made coffee that late morning and heartily ate scrambled eggs and bacon with toast and then fired up half a joint left over from the night before. He sat down at the kitchen nook by the window and sipped coffee slowly. Jesse could see the green water of the lake on both sides of the causeway. Whitecaps roiled in a strong wind that had gotten up early that morning and had only gotten stronger. The trees cut most of the wind to size by the time it reached him and only stirred the smaller limbs overhanging the trailer; but one limb insisted on a rhythmic gnawing of the trailer's roof and after a while he fetched a hacksaw and climbed awkwardly on the roof and sawed it off.

When the half-joint became a roach, he tossed it in an ashtray with others and rolled a new one expertly between his thumbs and forefingers and smoked it, slowly, with pleasure, and watched the occasional car creep across the causeway road. The road began at the far end of the lake where the county road that fed into it was hidden behind a low ridge. The sleepy town of Argus, Illinois, was five miles up that road. A car would abruptly emerge from behind the ridge on the far end as merely a distant, crawling shape, like an insect, but by the time it had crossed the lake and reached the deep, loose gravel that had accumulated like a sandbar at the intersection, Jesse could stare almost directly into the car and see the driver's face quite well before it turned left or right. A left turn took cars parallel to his woods, and when he was stoned during the night the abrupt sound of a car — passing slowly or stopping, especially — became exaggerated in his mind and he would wait in a paranoid rush to see if it turned onto his lane or kept going. There were regulars who came out to buy dope and maybe some speed or hash — nothing heavy, he had promised himself — and he knew who was who and their cars and fretted when a strange one merely used his lane to turn around.

It was midweek and there wouldn't be much traffic. Sometimes a farmer crossed the causeway with a tractor and plow, or Jesse would see a lumbering truck carrying heating oil for the smattering of fancy lake houses at the north end of the lake, where the Argus gentry lived. Argus Lake was surrounded by farm country and was the result of the damming of the Rich River to the west, near Bloomington-Normal, where he was from and had briefly attended Illinois State University; but he had flunked out after a year from lack of interest and too many keggers and had retreated to the trailer and stayed stoned and supported himself by selling dope to college kids and Argus townies. He kept his mouth shut when he went to town for supplies and kept as low a profile as he could anywhere else and waited for whatever was coming next.

Whatever was to come next would have to come across that causeway and so watching it had become as routine as the way some people watched television. Jesse was stuck in neutral with little interest in even finding a new gear. It was April, 1970, and he was a healthy and even strapping, long-haired boy-man of twenty, good-looking and six-foot, but the numbers and letters that counted above all else were the 2S that had dissolved into 1A after he flunked out, and his draft lottery number, 21, which was piss-poor low and he guessed almost certainly a guaranteed visit to Vietnam. He hadn't really checked that out, but felt it was probably just a matter of time. He didn't read newspapers very much and didn't have a TV, but he heard bits and pieces from people and suspected the war was raging pretty good. But did Nixon even know where he lived?

After breakfast he popped open a can of Pabst and turned on the powerful Marantz stereo. Loud music was one of the benefits of living isolated in woods, though he'd learned to keep it low at night when the music could impair his ability to hear a car come up his lane. He listened to the Stones' Exile on Main Street, then Jimi Hendrix growling All Along the Watchtower. But he got restless and then bored with the music and turned it off and drank another Pabst. He could always listen to music and decided to exercise some restraint, but wasn't sure why.

He also decided against getting drunk because he had the night before and so he brushed his teeth and washed his face and under his arms and put on a clean Chicago Bears sweatshirt before firing up another joint to keep the edge going. He dumped himself in the battered recliner and smoked the doobie and gazed out the window at the lake and causeway. Breakfast had swept the hangover away and he felt decent again. In his head he inventoried his latest deals, what was pending, what was on hand, what was coming, and felt satisfied he was money enough ahead to cruise for a while.

The dope business was self-perpetuating. It involved risk, but so far he had been lucky. He needed very little except food and beer and paid a small power bill each month. He hated phones and didn't have one. Who would he call? For a while he did have a girlfriend, a willowy, sweet little doper — Clarice — from Argus, fresh out of high school with long, straight blonde hair down to her tight ass, which filled her faded bell bottoms supremely well. She went off to college in Chicago one day to study art — with a fresh dope supply, of course — and that was that. Even if he had a phone, he knew she wouldn't be calling. Besides, customers knew how to find him. The trailer belonged to his uncle in Iowa, who assumed Jesse was still in college, and Jesse didn't disabuse him of the notion and sent him a modest rent check each month and some bullshit chitchat to notify him he was still kicking and to keep him from prying.

He settled into the chair and fell asleep for a few hours, and when he woke up he slowly became aware of a tiny speck moving onto the causeway at the far end. It moved too slow and was too small to be a car, of course, and soon he recognized the shape of a man wearing a pack and leaning hard into his stride to offset the wind. Jesse could not recall ever seeing a person walk across the causeway. It was an odd sight to him. It didn't belong. After a while, as the man crossed the little bridge midway that allowed boats access from each section of the lake, Jesse began to fret about the man and his steady, determined gait — the man marched, for God's sake. It was out of routine, out of place, and anything out of place and unexpected made him fearful. Jesse watched closely as the man's face came into focus as he inched closer and walked directly toward the woods and trailer and neared the intersection. He seemed to be walking straight at Jesse and looking directly at him, though Jesse knew the man could not see him. Still, he instinctively slid away from the window a little.

The man stopped at the intersection and looked right, then left. Right went past farms until it found a tiny burg called Kelton clustered around a grain elevator. Left went past the trailer and snaked around low rolling hills until it ended at a T intersection and no town or even houses nearby. The man took off his pack and leaned it against the metal guard railing of the road and then leaned himself against the railing and sagged from fatigue and the strain of fighting the wind. He produced a canteen and drank heartily, wiping his mouth with the sleeve of his jacket. Then he lit a cigarette. The blue smoke was visible from the trailer. The man smoked leisurely and looked around, at the lake, up at the sky, which was clearing, the sun trying to emerge; he leaned against the railing a good long time and sometimes looked straight ahead, at the trailer. He didn't seem to be in a hurry. He rummaged through his pack and ate something from it. Once he turned his back to the trailer and placed one foot on the railing and rested an elbow on his knee and appeared to survey the lake, to perhaps gauge how far he'd just walked to cross it.

Jesse grabbed the binoculars hanging on a nail by the refrigerator and studied the man intently. His hair was short, his face clean-shaven. Short hair stood out. Just about everyone Jesse associated with had varying degrees of long hair and moustaches and beards and sideburns. It was the new style, for a new time, Jesse vaguely thought. Only a few of the redneck Argus townies still had crew cuts. He looked through the binoculars again: the man's age was hard to gauge, too. Jesse thought he might be in his late twenties, then again maybe older. He looked athletic, lean. The face was tan, and that stood out to Jesse. No one had a tan in Argus in April unless they had been somewhere else to get it. Jesse studied the face more: he had never seen the man before. Jesse had become good at remembering faces quickly. It was a required skill of his trade.

The man flicked the cigarette butt into the lake and re-shouldered his pack. He looked again right, then left, and his glance lingered on a grove of trees along the lakeshore — almost exactly straight across the road from Jesse's trailer. He checked his watch and studied the grove again. He seemed to be assessing it. Finally he lurched across the road, stepped over the guardrail, and walked down the gentle slope toward the lake and into the grove, where Jesse lost sight of him. Jesse scanned the grove slowly, patiently, but could not find him. He waited, looked again, but still did not catch sight of him. He began to wonder if the man had gone on past the grove, along the lakeshore recessed out of sight, to make his way down that side of the lake. Jesse did not know what end that direction would produce because there were no houses there, just more woods all the way to the dam. Having the man unaccounted for was troubling.

When the man still didn't emerge from the grove, Jesse stepped outside his trailer with the binoculars to try to get a better look. He contemplated climbing to the trailer's roof, debated whether he might be too stoned to do it, but then he glimpsed the man finally, his pack off, rummaging around the grove; and Jesse saw him walk down to the edge of the lake and look out over it for a few minutes, smoking another cigarette. Then the man disappeared into the grove again and did not come out. The rest of the afternoon Jesse kept watch but did not see him. He didn't understand what the man was up to and wondered vaguely if the man was a threat. After working through his paranoia, he grudgingly decided he wasn't. A few minutes later he wasn't so sure; but still, he was something new in Jesse's carefully-ordered universe and could not simply be ignored. It was as if there was a door open somewhere that needed to be closed.

Jesse was pretty sure the man wasn't a cop. It made no sense for a cop to truck a pack across that damn long causeway. Cops rode in comfort and came with the band playing, not dragging packs on their backs. The man could be a drifter, but that seemed odd because his clothes looked clean and not worn; the pack was a good one with a sturdy frame and not cheap by the look of it. The man was clean-shaven and not scraggly. Drifters wouldn't be likely to stray away from the interstate on the far side of Argus where they could find rides north to Chicago or south to St. Louis. Drifters often weren't clothed for any real weather and this man had a good jacket and Jesse had seen a bedroll wedged between his neck and pack so it didn't chafe and rode comfortably. The man appeared confident in his stride. Wherever it was he was going, to Jesse it seemed he knew the way.

As night began to creep in, Jesse positioned his recliner so he could look out a window facing the grove. He decided he couldn't fix any dinner — leftover cold Kentucky Fried Chicken and baked beans at best — until he felt the man was somehow accounted for. So he kept watching and frowned at the approaching darkness. He had contemplated just walking across the road and saying hello, but dismissed the idea: you didn't just walk up on someone in a grove of trees with it almost dark. The margin of error was too high. All sorts of things could go wrong. Maybe the man had a gun, too. Maybe he would interpret Jesse as a sudden threat. That was one of the things that could go haywire in a hurry. To hell in a hand basket. To the shits in a shingle. Jesse heard himself saying those things out loud and decided to lay off the dope. At least until this man in the grove business was resolved.

Finally, it was dark and Jesse reluctantly flipped the switch to turn on the light above the trailer's door. There were no other lights on either side of the road. Night was always very black out there, and he knew the man could not miss seeing his light. Would he come over? If the man had not noticed the trailer during daylight, then he would surely be very curious about a light in the woods. If he did come calling, what would happen? Jesse did not believe the man was someone intending to commit mayhem of some sort. But that was just a gut feeling. Wishful thinking, perhaps.

Soon Jesse saw the orange glow of a campfire in the grove.

"I'll be go to hell," Jesse said. "Piss up a rope. A camp-fucking-fire."

Jesse wondered briefly how the man had managed to scrounge enough wood, but then accepted for the time being that he had moved in and meant to stay awhile. Hell, he was setting up camp, setting up shop, moving into the damn neighborhood. Jesse retrieved the bucket of chicken from the fridge and munched it slowly, spooned cold baked beans to his mouth, and glanced from time to time at the grove and the steady glow of the fire. The man evidently stirred it with a stick and tossed a chunk of wood in because it flared up like a big blowtorch and Jesse saw sparks rising from it like mad fireflies.

"Now he's got her cooking. Cookin' like a motherfucker."

Jesse wondered why he'd never made a campfire of his own. He had the space and the privacy. The trailer sat in a clearing ringed by trees. He could have made one real easy. There was plenty of dead wood around that he could have collected. But collecting wood would have seemed like work to him — had he ever thought of it at all — and he knew that probably was why a fire never occurred to him.

Or had he somehow lost his imagination? He didn't think so. He felt he could imagine some pretty wild things. Had the dope done something to him? He'd read that marijuana was pretty much harmless. And it had some health benefits, someone had told him once. He didn't know if that was true or not. But it sure did make him good and shit-faced and what harm was there in that?

Jesse turned back to look at the campfire glow again. What was the man going to eat for dinner? He had food with him. Had to. No one would carry a heavy damn pack for miles without something worth the trouble. He could have all sorts of stuff in there: canned goods, like chili and fruit cocktail — some cans of SPAM, Vienna sausages, stuff like that. He'd need one of those dinky frying pans that didn't take up much space but were big enough to fry SPAM slices or whatever. He could have some bacon with him. Jesse felt he would take some bacon along if he were in the man's shoes. If the man had money enough, he might have even bought himself a nice steak in Argus just for that night's meal. If it fit his travel budget, that is. But they could wrap that steak in plastic real good and tight and it would travel just fine until he cooked it because it wasn't warm weather yet. But a frozen steak would have been even smarter and Jesse congratulated himself for thinking of it. He still had a good imagination. That was proof. Yep — just buy a frozen steak in Argus at Ferguson's IGA, and by the time you'd walked out to the lake and built the fire — presto, that steak is thawed and ready to sizzle and pop and spurt its juices over the fire.

Or maybe the man didn't have much at all. Some candy bars, maybe. Maybe the plan was to amble over in the morning and try and mooch off him. Would he feed the man? He shook his head at the thought: of course he would. He wouldn't turn away anyone who was hungry as long as he had means of his own. He'd let customers crash sometimes on his sofa when they had no place to go that night. But he'd always made sure the dope stash was under control first. That was his business. That was prudent. He wondered if the man would understand that. Whatever the man's business was, he surely had his own code for running it. Even if he was a drifter, there was a code for that, too.

Jesse glanced at the grove. Could the man even see his trailer light at all through the campfire? It looked like a real barnburner. On a cool night it would be just the ticket. Sitting around a fire with a beer, maybe some chili — that worked pretty well. He had plenty of Pabst in the fridge. Should he grab a six and go on over, maybe break the ice? It was tempting. Maybe he'd even like having a neighbor; but the man wasn't a true neighbor. Not without a roof over his head. Jesse checked to make sure he had a cold six of PBR, but standing there, looking in the fridge, he realized nothing had changed. Going over at night was risky. Maybe dangerous. With that roaring campfire, the man would not be able to hear him come up, probably — nor see him until he was right on him practically and that could cause big problems. Big-time fucking problems. No, that wasn't going to do. He could have a gun in his pack, or under his jacket. Even if he wasn't some killer or dildo jerk on a jack-off lark of some kind, he could still be a fool with a gun who might take things the wrong way. He might think Jesse was a homo, for example. Or a cop. Or a territorial farmer with a shotgun. All manner of things could happen. It could be a nasty fucking world out there if you didn't have your shit wired tight.

So instead, Jesse did nothing more than finish eating and then cleaned up his kitchen. He filled a bag with trash and took it outside to be hauled into town and dumped. The glow of the campfire, though, was still tempting. He saw the man get up once, then sit down again. The man got up a few minutes later and was out of sigh for a few more minutes — probably had to piss, Jesse thought. Should he just walk down his lane for a better look? He even took a few steps that way. He paused, then walked some more. He could be down the lane and across the road just like that. Thirty seconds or so. Maybe a minute. But, no, that was foolish. An impulse. Impulses could get you hurt, could get you killed. He retreated to the trailer and locked the door. That was prudent, he reminded himself. He even switched off the outside light, but a minute later switched it back on, worried that if the man had seen it on he would be concerned or suspicious when it went out. In his fluctuating paranoia, Jesse also fretted that turning it back on would prompt the man to come for a look; but switching it off yet gain could make it even more of a distraction to be investigated, so he stuck with leaving it on. Then he turned it off one more time and back on again and left it alone, finally, though he glanced at the switch several times.

Jesse didn't know what to do with himself at first. He walked back to the bedroom and then checked his bathroom. He picked up a few dirty towels from the floor and tossed them in a laundry basket. He looked at his face in the mirror. He needed to shave, but decided to wait until morning, before he went to town. He would wash his hair in the morning, too. Jesse straightened up his small living room to keep himself busy, distracted. He made a list of supplies to get at the grocery store. He usually wasn't that organized, but figured maybe it was time to get with the program.

When he had run out of housekeeping things to do, he settled in the recliner and turned on the stereo — low, at first, but by the snarling heat of the Stones' Gimme Shelter, he cranked it.

Oh, a storm is threatening
My very life today
If I don't get some shelter
Oh yeah, I'm gonna fade away

War, children, it's just a shot away
It's just a shot away
War, children, it's just a shot away
It's just a shot away

His body began to sway with the music. When it had its hook into him good and deep, Jesse said, "Fuck it."

He rolled a joint and fired it up. Inhaled deeply. Exhaled slowly. Watched the smoke curl lazily toward the ceiling. When the dope's magic had once again enveloped him in that silky warm blanket of fog, he forgot to look over at the campfire at all.

2.

Raul

Raul wasn't his real name. That was just what he crowned himself after he escaped high school and enlisted, with only a perpetual boner and $27 in his pants. He liked the sound of Raul, the way it rolled off the tongue, especially when he drank too much and he slurred it slowly to irritate whoever he was with. Dominick Cruikshank was his real name. Dominick Artemis Cruikshank, for Christ's sake. His mother liked Dominick and Artemis equally and couldn't decide, and so his parents had flipped a coin and the order was established. He wasn't Italian at all, though some people assumed it because of his names. He was in fact pretty much of British descent — the family insisted on a skinny link of sorts to George Cruikshank, an English caricaturist of some repute and notoriety — with a sprinkling of Cherokee from some Indian buck who'd shinnied up his family tree after the Trail of Tears. Or before it. That wasn't clear to him.

As for deciding on Raul — it just came to him impulsively after reading about Che Guevara and Fidel Castro and learning Castro's bro was a Raul. That and wanting to stand out with something short and blunt and in your face, thank you very fucking much, without the rather lengthy Dominick Artemis Cruikshank to throw around. He always felt it made him sound like a snotty-nosed pussy from New Yawk City.

Raul stoked the embers of the sleeping campfire with a stick and skillfully brought it back to a roaring life. He unwrapped bacon and put four slices in a small skillet and balanced it on two pieces of smoldering wood. Ferguson's IGA in Argus had cut the bacon good and thick, with a generous balance between fat and meat, and he was grateful because he was very hungry. Old Man Ferguson had cut the slices himself, a nod to a fellow war vet. When the bacon began cracking and popping and had lubricated the skillet, he cracked open two eggs and dropped them in a corner of the skillet and listened happily to them sizzle. It was a cool morning and he had slept well in his sleeping bag by the fire.

Once in the night he had awakened with a start and reached for a weapon that wasn't there. He felt groggy and the night cold confused him — corn-fused, Argus townies would call it. The sounds weren't right — there were no sounds except a gentle breeze scrubbing treetops with a quiet moan and the gentle lapping of water on the nearby shore. When he realized where he was, his breathing slowed to normal. He watched the moon being tickled by passing clouds for a long time, made an uneasy peace of sorts with the awful near-silence of home, and had fallen asleep again very soundly.

He warmed his hands close to the flames and listened to the bacon crackle and the eggs talk back to him, too. He spooned instant coffee into his metal cup and filled it with water from the canteen and wedged it among glowing embers. He eased the skillet back from the fire and let everything cook slower. He closed his eyes for a moment. He wanted to hear and smell the eggs and bacon. He held off his hunger as best he could just to savor the aroma and the sound of popping juices.

While he sipped his coffee carefully, he stood up a moment for a look across the road. There was some doofus living across the way in a shitty little trailer. He'd heard loud music coming from there all night — some Stones, some Who, the Beatles, and even some Jefferson Airplane. He had good taste in tunes — give him that much. Whoever the dickhead was, though, he liked to play with his outside light switch. It had flashed on and off a bunch of times. Maybe the guy was signaling spaceships for a landing. Or it was part of some goofy cult involving dead animals and drinking blood. You never knew what you might get out deep in the country with some trailer trash hermit.

Or maybe he was a hippie, judging by the music. Not that Raul had a damn thing against hippies. He didn't. He'd broke bread with plenty of them in Haight-Ashbury, out in San Fran, when he was discharged. Most hippies he met were cool, friendly — stoned to the gills, but what else was new. He'd spent a month out there (told his folks by phone he owed the Army another month) until money ran low, just hanging out, smoking weed, pitching in a few dollars for wine and food at whoever's pad he crashed, and grooving to good bands, like the Jefferson Airplane, Moby Grape, Grateful Dead. He had been awfully sorry that Janis Joplin had died. Hendrix, too. Purple Haze had sort of been his theme song back in the Big Green Machine — the soggy jungles of Vietnam.

That month seemed like a decade ago. When his wake-up to go back to the world finally arrived, he was deposited in San Fran and told, you're free now, so go on and pretend none of this happened — if you can, Jack — and thanks very fucking much (just a dream, Jack), and marry that high school sweetheart/cheerleader with big tits, if she ain't fucking your best friend from the football team, who went to college while you humped in country, and try to sleep again in a dry bed with clean sheets (silk, Jack) with no ordnance cooking off in the background, no zips trying to zap you, no walking point, no humping for all she's worth and then some, no dinky-dao this or dinky-dao that, and get a boring job making widgets or shuffling papers or fixing mufflers or counting toilet plungers at K-mart (ask about the retirement plan, Jack), and get back on that meat and potatoes diet to accelerate the hardening of your arteries, and have a merry fucking nice damn life and one day read about where you were in a history book with your kids and scratch your head (but not your balls, Jack) wondering if it really happened at all. Just a movie, Jack. Just a late night John Wayne fucking movie.

He drifted home to Argus to visit his folks, who were a little afraid of him because he didn't quite look like or sound like the boy they had watched leave for the Army: his table manners were sloppy — atrocious, really — and he cussed a lot: fucking A or fucking this, fucking that. In San Fran he had stayed drunk or stoned or both much of the time and dropped a few dollars on strippers for blowjobs at first, then he graduated to the whole enchilada with a couple hookers down in the Tenderloin, and except for the absence of people shooting at him, and the welcome sight of round-eye pussy everywhere, it was a little like still being in a more expensive Saigon with much better weather. But Argus had struck him as too slow motion of a landscape and after a few days of playing returning hero with his proud father at the VFW and with his mother at Cameron's Cafe, he loaded his pack and set off for the lake. He just needed some time, he figured — and some space.

Raul poured more water and instant coffee in his cup and nestled it back among the embers for a few minutes to boil. He sat back on his haunches the way the dinks did back in the Green Machine and recalled the hump out from Argus — only five miles from town and maybe a mile across the causeway, which wasn't much for a guy used to humping all day through thick saw grass, sometimes in monsoon rain, sometimes just humidity so bad it soaked you as thoroughly as the monsoons, and you didn't walk in it so much as you swam it. But already he was a little out of shape thanks to his month in San Fran doing nothing and his hips were actually a little sore from the previous day's hump.

Cool weather took some getting used to, but he liked it, didn't realize how much he'd missed it. The hump out was along a mostly level county road (real blacktop, no army craters, Jack) cutting through soybean and cornfields like a zipper. A few farms, neat and orderly. Crops beginning to sprout. Hardly a car on the road. Everything looking healthy. No B-52s cruising silently above. No blackened stretches of napalm-scorched earth. No choppers overhead with rotors beating crazily. No mortar rounds plunging in. And it was the quiet that struck him most. Dead silence, almost, with only a few chatty sparrows in trees. A hawk circled silently and vigilantly overhead. Once his quick eyes caught movement in the ditch and instincts and fear grabbed him pretty good, but it was only a pair of male pheasants with that breathtaking plumage moving fast but silently to stay ahead of him like Charlie did back in the Green.

He hadn't had a bad war, all things considered. Not getting shot and killed was the very top of his list of good things to be concluded from it. A bullet or two did come close, and one, a heavy round from an AK-47, singed the fabric of his sleeve just enough to gouge a small hole but not deep enough to touch the skin — you didn't have to fall into the Grand Canyon, Raul joked to his platoon mates, to say you'd seen the damn thing. In high school Raul had read about soldiers in the Civil War who ended a battle without wounds, but discovered holes in their hats and coats and dents in a sword's scabbard or an ammunition box and they knew just how close was the line between a good day and your last day. Like with pilots who believed any landing you walked away from was a good one, Raul had learned the universal soldier's axiom that a miss was as good as a mile.

His war had actually been pleasant sometimes because most of his tour was spent guarding a supply dump near Saigon that got rocketed a few times, but fairly inaccurately at first, though Charlie's aim improved over time and there were plenty of near things to laugh nervously about over a joint and beer later. He got into Saigon often and fucked pretty girls with long silky hair at Madame Thou's establishment and drank lots of that rotgut beer (church keys required, even though pop tops were common in the states — back in the world, Jack) that supposedly had formaldehyde in it. Got a head start on the embalming, he guessed, and even sometimes Raul veered away from the whorehouse and instead visited colorful markets and Buddhist temples. But usually he could be found with buddies in sleazy bars catering to GIs and drinking Carling Black Label or Biere 33 or Biere Larue in a one-liter bottle.

He only had to hump the bush one time, for a couple weeks late in his tour, when units were short and replacements were scrounged from security details at bases near Saigon. That was when the AK round sought him out so tenaciously. He heard it go by like a loud and angry hornet. He'd felt it along his sleeve and, in his anxiety and fear and combat paranoia, had assumed he'd been hit and had yelled that to no one in particular, then felt very stupid and embarrassed when a medic glanced at his sleeve and rolled his eyes and handed him the M-16 he'd dropped on his foot, which produced real pain, unlike the AK round.

"No purple heart, troop, for dropping your weapon on your fucking foot," the medic had hissed.

But nonetheless, Raul had seen The Elephant, got his cherry busted, and became a card-carrying member of The Club. It certainly seemed to mean a lot to his old man when they visited the VFW. World War II and Korea vets would nod at him like they were all fraternity brothers, but Raul felt he was like a member who never learned the secret handshake.

Raul didn't think he had killed anybody, though he'd certainly fired off a lot of rounds, those supersonic 5.56 mm bullets that tumbled and rocketed out of the barrel and reached obscene speed before tearing into something, usually palm trees or brush or the dirt. Maybe he'd hit someone and maybe he hadn't. No way to know. Sometimes he knew he fired off a clip that had no chance of hitting much besides air because he hurried and didn't aim and was just spraying like a fool, the clip emptying in an instant. It sounded reassuring but wasn't doing much good and some burly sergeant had thumped the back of his helmet hard with a meaty paw and barked, "Goddamnit, troop — direct your fucking fire."

He never once saw Charlie except lined up dead for a body count. Shattered bodies that didn't look like they ever could have been alive and so formidable — and so damn fucking elusive — in the deep green jungle. Then the channel got changed — just like that, Jack — and he was choppered out of the Green to a waiting C-130 for the

Philippines, then Hawaii, and San Fran. He had a layover
in Manila and he stayed drunk and tried out the girls at
a local establishment. In Hawaii he walked along Waikiki
Beach, but discovered the price was much higher and the
girls much more clinical and distant and business-like than
in the Nam — but it was round-eye and very much like a
rediscovered treasure.

The eggs and bacon were ready and he ate them right
out of the skillet with great pleasure. Breakfast in a café just
didn't have the same edge as over an open fire. You couldn't
get the smoke in a café or restaurant. In a café you were
hemmed in and surrounded by the awful sound of clanging
silverware and plates and cups and country music and you
just couldn't concentrate as well on how the eggs swam in
bacon juices and the bacon's crisp texture melted into the
coffee in his mouth to make something better than just the
two by themselves. He pulled a slice of bread from a bag in
the pack and mopped up the skillet with it and ate it slowly,
chewing well, and it was almost like a second breakfast.
After he swallowed the last of the bread soaked in juices, he
impulsively put two more thick slices of bacon in the skillet
and cooked them quickly and not quite fully, with much fat
left but that was his goal. He scooped the bacon onto a slice
of bread and folded it and then got up and ate it slowly as
he walked down to the shore of the lake.

By the shore he finished the bacon sandwich — he
should have stuck a small jar of mayonnaise in his pack, he
lamented — and licked his fingers and felt very satisfied.
There was no wind and the lake's surface was glass stretching
all the way south, to the dam more than a mile away. In
high school he used to make out with girls at the dam until
a county mountie would come along, headlights blazing
right into his car, and make them zip up and move on. It

seemed like another life, another person. He watched the lake's surface a long time, then remembered to fetch the skillet and rinse it in the water. Raul brushed his teeth and washed his face with a bar of soap. The cold lake water on his face was bracing and made him feel clean as much as the soap did. Back in his camp he hung his pack on a tree knot and made another cup of coffee.

After a while he looked across the road and saw a blonde, longhair stirring clumsily around the trailer carrying chunks of wood and making his own campfire. Raul was in no hurry. He sipped his coffee and watched the longhair disappear and re-appear carrying wood. The longhair looked over at him several times. When Raul had come back from washing up at the lakeshore, he had noticed the longhair's fire roaring, a vicious black cloud still mushrooming into the tree canopy (like napalm, Jack), and wondered how the dipshit had gotten the fire going so quickly. Maybe he knew his ass from a hole in the ground after all and wasn't some hippie numbnuts. Might be a real woodsman over there. A regular Paul Fucking Bunyan. You just never knew.

Soon Raul would walk over and see what the dipshit was all about. But there just wasn't any hurry.

None in the world.

3.

Jesse

Jesse had stupidly used gas — and way too much of it — to start his campfire. It erupted in a blinding, whooshing, orange flash, singing his eyebrows and some hairs in his bangs. He had somehow thrown himself away from the explosion in time, but it scared the holy fucking shit out of him. Jesse climbed awkwardly to his feet, brushing dirt from the knees of his jeans, and trembled for a few minutes. He fumbled for a joint in his jacket pocket and fired it up to console himself. He shivered in the morning coolness out of reach of the fire's heat for a few more minutes before the dope helped him make peace with how close he'd come to burning his face off.

He looked across the road to check whether the man had seen him nearly blow himself up, but didn't see him anywhere. That was good. Very good. Jesse shook his head at how careless he'd been. Jesus H. Christ. The man would have taken him for a dangerous fool, no doubt. Jesse had seen the man only once that morning, while he lugged wood to build his own fire, and the man had stood up and seemed to be looking over at him, but Jesse couldn't be sure. Maybe he was just stretching his legs. The man already had his fire going. An early bird. Maybe he'd even eaten breakfast. Jesse thought he'd smelled bacon, faintly, when he got dressed and went outside. Jesse had been tempted to wave when he saw the man, but stopped himself, fearing it might seem kind of goofy, or even girlish.

Jesse pulled the metal grill itself off his barbecue grill and placed it across the burning logs, congratulating himself on his ingenuity; but he neglected to balance the grill evenly and after he'd cracked eggs into the skillet, it spilled and he had to start over. The second time he tried to make scrambled eggs, but forgot to use oil and the eggs cooked too fast into a hardened yellow mass. He finally gave up on eggs and warmed the last few pieces of the Kentucky Fried Chicken in the skillet and washed it down with PBR. Breakfast of Champions, he snickered, though he wished he had eggs and bacon instead, maybe some orange juice, too. He vowed to go into town and make himself shop responsibly. He would get some T-bones and some potatoes and dinner would get done right. Some wine, too — not just Ripple or Boone's Farm, but maybe some of that Blue Nun or Liebfraumilch. The good stuff.

After he ate, he pulled a lawn chair by the fire and got comfortable. The fire had settled into a steady orange and blue burn. Jesse recalled his brush with it and laughed. He had a decent buzz going and was having a hard time motivating himself to go into town. He needed stuff. There was almost nothing left to eat except for some Campbell's soup; but it was so easy, so tempting, just to sit by the fire and do nothing but space out. The fire was better than television and he stared into it, watching flames dance and lick at the wood. It was better even than staring at a poster of Elvis or a sailing ship under one of those black lights. He made a mental note to go to the head shop in Bloomington and look for one of those lights. There were people there he could do some business with, too. A man had to work and make a living.

When Jesse finally looked up from the fire, he saw the man sauntering up his lane. He resisted the powerful temptation to panic and maybe leap from his chair. He knew that could be seen as standoffish, defensive. You didn't want people to know you had something to hide. The temptation was fueled by fear exerting a very real sort of gravitational pull that had to be resisted or he might be vaulted into space. He didn't know this man. He had a business to run that didn't get advertised in newspapers or the yellow pages, for God's sake, and so he had to be careful with strangers. Everyone was a stranger until they proved to be something else. Even then you watched your back. He gripped the cedar arm rails of the chair and held on. Wipe the shitty grin off the face, he told himself. Get it together. Appear strong. Be confident. Be friendly, but not an open book. Wire your shit up tight and keep it tight. Smile — no, don't smile; that's goofy. Set the jaw. Appear calm. Appear strong, but not too tough. Yes, that was it.

The man was just yards away, his stride fluid, arms swinging freely at his sides and not stuffed into pockets, which Jesse would have viewed as a sort of misdirection mode of some kind. The man seemed to him to be at ease. He wasn't smiling, yet his face seemed on the verge of it. He might be one of those who smile quickly, easily. You could tell a lot about someone by how they moved and Jesse concluded that this one tended toward openness rather than concealment. But you couldn't be sure and you never bet the farm on strangers if the stakes mattered at all.

"Howdy," the man said. His voice was firm and baritone, but not menacing.

"Hey," Jesse said, and he was immediately sorry that it sounded squeaky.

The man stopped a yard short of Jesse — Midwest etiquette required an honorable acknowledgment of personal space. He glanced briefly at the fire. His face still seemed neutral to Jesse.

"That's quite a fire you got there, troop."

"Troop" just slipped out. Force of habit.

The word was foreign to Jesse. He didn't quite know how to take it, but sensed it wasn't a threat — maybe it was a new variation of man or dude or brother or friend. He decided to let it go and see if it came back or just disappeared. To probe it right off the bat would seem too investigative. You had to know what to question and what to just watch float downstream under the bridge.

"I worked on it all morning," Jesse said, a subtle attempt at humor and he would see if the man followed his drift.

The man's eyes brightened just a little. "Say you did?"

Jesse liked the reply. It had plenty of wiggle room and wasn't judgmental, though playful.

"Naw," Jesse said, offering the first smile of the engagement. "I used some gas."

The man recalled the black mushroom cloud and nodded, noting Jesse was a candidate to be a numbnuts, but at least he was an honest numbnuts. Maybe something to build on.

"I'm Raul." He offered a hand and they shook. Raul's grip was stronger.

"Jesse." He chewed on the odd name for a moment. Raul. "I saw you come in last night."

"Yeah," Raul said. "I noticed your trailer, but by the time I got squared away over there, it was near dark. Didn't want to startle anyone by just hoofin' it on over."

Jesse noted that the first awkward moment had arrived. He had expected it.

"Comfy over there?" Jesse finally said, regretting immediately the use of comfy. It was a pussy word — did he think the man had checked into a Holiday Inn?

"It's not bad. It's OK, really. I've seen a lot worse, believe me." Raul altered their course a couple degrees. "Heard your stereo last night. It serenaded me to sleep."

"Too loud, man?"

"Not at all. Sound carries nicely out here in the boonies. You played my kind of stuff, man. I appreciated the Jeff Airplane you got around to. I saw them last month in San Fran."

"Really?" Jesse was impressed and sat up a little in his chair. "You want to sit down, man? There's another chair folded against the trailer. Pull it up, if you like."

"Believe I will."

Instead of pulling the chair open, Raul clutched it hard by the back brace, gave a sharp snap with his wrist, and it shot open. A neat move, Jesse thought. Broke the ice nicely. He still didn't have a sharp bead on who Raul was, but he knew he wasn't a cop and didn't feel he was some other kind of monkey maybe dragging trouble around behind him. A drifter, maybe, but more likely a drifter with someplace to go and just trying to get there. It made a difference, and that stuff about seeing the Jeff Airplane was certainly in Raul's favor. Raul — he'd never met anyone called that.

"Raul, that's your real name, man?"

Raul smiled. "That's just what I like to go by. Dominick is my real name. Dominick Cruikshank. Dominick Artemis Cruikshank. You see how that sounds? So, I shortened things up a bit."

"Jesse Archer." It was Jesse's turn to offer a hand and they shook again. Jesse put a tad more bite into his grip so as not to be outclassed. "There was a TV show with an Artemis. I remember it. Do you know the one I mean? Can't remember the name."

"The Wild, Wild West. James West and Artemis Gordon. My mom liked that show. She sometimes tried to call me Artie, like how James West called Artemis Artie, but I didn't let it take."

"Good move," Jesse said.

"I hear you. A guy can't go around labeled Artemis."

"That's true. But Artemis Gordon was sort of cool in a sissy kind of way. I mean, when it counted, he stood up, and all that. He saved Jim's butt a few times."

"Sure he did. But Jim West was a stud. Kicked ass and took names.

"Yeah he did," Jesse nodded gravely. "You didn't fuck with James West."

"Not even a little bit," Raul said. "Remember that dwarf character — Miguelito?"

Jesse strained to recall it, then got it in decent focus. "Oh, yeah — he could make time slow down, right?"

"But Jim nailed his ass just the same."

"True. There's no denying it."

More silence for a minute.

"Where you from, Raul?"

"Argus, man. Just up the road."

"I'll be go to hell," Jesse said. "I'm from Bloomington. I had you pegged as from the west coast maybe."

"Nope. Born and raised in Argus. I'm a townie, dude."

"But not always," Jesse said. "You were out in California."

Raul blinked a couple times. "I came back through California, through San Fran."

"Back from where?"

"The Nam, man. Viet Fucking Nam."

"Oh." That shut Jesse up for a minute. And the use of "troop" suddenly made sense.

"Ain't nothing," Raul said. "It's just a place on the map, a colored shape on the globe."

"A state of mind," Jesse said absently.

"What?"

"I remember hearing someone say Vietnam is just a state of mind. I read it, I think. Must have been in a newspaper. I don't have TV out here."

"Who said that?" Raul said. "Someone who'd been there, right? Had to be, because that's a good way to put it. The Nam is definitely a fucking state of mind alright."

Jesse suddenly remembered his piss-poor lottery number, but with some effort managed not to think about it deeply. It was what it was. But he wasn't sure what to say. Remembering the other joint in his jacket, he produced it and stuck it in his mouth.

"So, you want to share a doobie, man — to celebrate getting home and all that shit?"

"Sounds like a wiener to me." Raul produced a wooden match in a quick motion from his own jacket and ignited it expertly between his thumb and forefinger. Another cool move. Jesse leaned over and let Raul put the flame to the joint's tip. A show of trust.

"That's some good shit," Raul said, exhaling a cloud of smoke.

"I know it. You can't buy better weed anywhere in this part of the state, I reckon."

"It's been a couple weeks since I toked anything like this, Jesse. I'm fucked up, man."

"Time for a beer. You want a PBR, Raul?"

"Does a bear shit in the woods?"

"Right — is the pope Catholic?"

"Exactly, man — does a fat dog fart?"

"I never heard that one," Jesse said.

"Now you have, man."

Jesse fetched two PBRs and put Surrealistic Pillow on the stereo turntable. He dialed the volume about mid-level and left the trailer door open.

"I love the Jeff Airplane," Raul said. "That's a cool fucking band."

"For sure. Beats hell out of that Carpenters shit — you won't find that in my eight-track anytime soon."

"Or the Osmonds," Raul said.

"Man, I hate the Osmonds. And the Jackson Five."

"It's killing real rock, dude," Raul said.

"Oh, yeah. It's criminal. So, Raul, what's your favorite Airplane tune?"

"White Rabbit, man. Yours?"

"Somebody to Love, I guess. Grace Slick has got some dynamite pipes on that one."

"I hear you. Good-looking babe, too."

"She's outrageous," Jesse said. "Boner material."

Raul smirked, raised his PBR can. "To boner material."

They clinked cans and then Jesse put the roach between the teeth of needle nose pliers and they snorted it.

"I'm buzzed," Jesse said.

"Fried, man."

"Shit-faced."

"Drilled," Raul said.

"Hammered."

"Consumed."

"Where's that one from — Nam?" Jesse said.

"The west coast. Heard it in San Fran."

"What do they say in Nam?"

"Help."

Jesse laughed and after a moment so did Raul.

"So, if the Wild, Wild West was still on, what kind of shit do you think they'd be doing?" Jesse said.

Raul contemplated it. "Well, far out stuff, I think. More of that slowing down time shit, for a fact."

"This dope slows time down pretty good, too."

Raul smirked like the Cheshire Cat. "Fucking A."

Jesse fidgeted in his chair. "I need to go to town some time and get some stuff. Interested in a road trip around the lake? I've got a couple new cassettes."

"You plan to walk?" Raul looked around. "You got a car, man?"

"Behind the trailer. Under a tarp."

"Really? You hide it?"

"I protect it from weather and shit. Falling branches. And if it ain't in sight from the road, people don't get tempted to mess with it."

Raul wiggled his lips. "You really think someone will mess with it? Out here? What is it, a Corvette or something?"

"I wish." Jesse laughed. "Naw, it's just a GTO."

Raul leaned forward in his chair. "There ain't no such thing as just a GTO. What year?"

"Sixty-seven."

"Whoa! Very cherry. Let's take a look."

When Jesse removed the tarp, Raul whistled softly. The GTO was red, a convertible, and indeed cherry. It had been waxed, the chrome wheels meticulously scrubbed by hand. Jesse knew it would be a sin not to take care of such a car.

"Bad-ass," Raul said. "Very bad-ass."

Jesse unexpectedly felt pride of ownership — pride of caring for something. He carefully backed the GTO out from behind the trailer and revved the 400 cid motor to impress Raul.

"A real cruiser," Raul said. "We're looking good, man. What new tapes you got?"

"Revolver and Sergeant Pepper. I just got them a few weeks ago."

"They're not new," Raul said.

"Well, I just got around to them. Better late than never."

Jesse slid Sergeant Pepper into the eight-track.

"Pepper's some deep shit, Jesse."

"That's what I'm thinking. A Day in the Life blows my mind."

They pulled onto the county blacktop and Jesse gunned it, leaving rubber and blue smoke. The GTO fishtailed a few seconds, then straightened and dug in and Jesse chopped the speed. They rumbled along with that big motor growling like it was some monstrous angry cat. They were silent all the way through Lucy in the Sky with Diamonds. Time really had seemed to slow to a crawl for them. At first Jesse forgot to crank the music a little to be heard over the motor.

"So, how do you afford this car, man?" Raul said. "Do you work?"

Jesse hesitated. He reminded himself that although Raul seemed cool, he was still new people. New people were sort of on probation until they demonstrated they could become old people, trustworthy people. So he massaged the truth. Like time, truth was flexible.

"I guess you'd say I'm between jobs," Jesse said. "Still got a few bucks. Bought the car from my uncle pretty cheap."

"A steal, right?"

"It ain't that big of a deal."

Raul nodded. "And you live out in the boonies, in a trailer, because, what — you love nature?"

Jesse glanced at him. "Yeah, something like that. I like hearing the birdies sing in the morning."

"Uh-huh," Raul said. "Very groovy — very mellow."

Jesse dug out another joint to try and change the subject.

"You seem to always have a joint," Raul said as he produced another wooden match and ignited it between thumb and forefinger.

"I'm lucky that way."

4.

Nicole

She didn't intend to be stuck punching a cash register in Ferguson's IGA forever. No way. Not if she had a thing to say about it at all. It was definitely and irreversibly Nowheresville with a cherry on top. Nicole Michelle Beckert had glimpsed the outside world through Life and Time magazines and the six o'clock news out of Bloomington. She'd heard firsthand accounts about the World Beyond the Flatlands from Argus refugees who had escaped its gravitational pull for lives in widescreen technicolor. College was the ticket. Maybe ISU — maybe even Illinois over in Champaign. She was a year out of high school and her grades had been very good. Sharp as a tack, people said. Already she had saved money by living at home. Her folks wanted her to try college, too, and so she figured to study psychology. Everyone she knew agreed she could size people up faster and better than most. She saw all kinds coming through her line and had learned quickly how to schmooze with everything from depression to outright belligerence. She was of a mind to try to capitalize on that and become a shrink, or a social worker at the very least. And not just in Bloomington or Champaign. Chicago wasn't so far up the road.

There just had to be more than ringing up eggs and sodas and rump roasts — those silly mood rings — and counting drawers and taking cigarette breaks behind the store among pimply-faced stock boys with scraggly sideburns who drooled and checked out her ass when they didn't think she would notice. Nicole was also tired of Friday night grabfests in some horndog's Chevelle SS 396 at the Stardust Drive-in while he fumbled like a gorilla in heat with her bra strap under her sweater and then licked her nipples with the finesse of a hungry goat. She didn't have anything against getting her nipples licked, but she was sure she could find a better skill level and maybe someone with some prospects in life.

At almost 5-10 — nearly 6-feet in heels — Nicole was what Argus folks called a tall drink of water. Certainly the stock boys — and even old Mr. Ferguson, she realized with great revulsion — desired a sip of her. She had almond-shaped eyes, thick black eyelashes, and long raven hair to the middle of her back. Often people said she resembled Cher, or teased her that she was an Indian maiden, which was OK with her as long as they didn't bring it up too often. The other cashiers were mostly short and dumpy with too much peroxide hair and bad complexions and so Nicole towered and was like a homing beacon to all the men who fumbled through her line, married or not.

She had babysat when she was younger for the Tates, neighbors and close friends of her folks, and one night the very gross Mr. Tate, a rather emaciated-looking man with hairy knuckles and nose hairs, had touched her ass as he helped her put on her coat to go home. Nicole said nothing about it until the next time she sat for their twins, when she quietly but firmly explained to Mr. Tate in the kitchen that if he ever touched her ass or any other part of her again she would surgically remove his testicles with a dull butter knife and feed them to his dog. Ever since then Mr. Tate always nervously avoided her line at the store. But plenty of men didn't.

Nicole didn't give it away. She didn't try to sell it, either. A man had to earn her treasures, as well as her goodwill, and she wouldn't tolerate lies. A couple cashiers had already got knocked-up thanks to sweet-talk without rubbers in the backseat of a car. That wasn't for Nicole. Pregnancy meant you officially were chained to Argus for the rest of your dreary life, married to some fool of a goober who would drink too much Budweiser and grow a flabby belly, and work at the local lumber yard — or as what they called a limberdick at Fleener's Hardware. A limberdick was a guy who barely graduated high school (but did great in shop class) and spent his life inventorying toilet supplies for Old Man Fleener, or counted fan belts and Pennzoil cans at Roger Gilstrap's Texaco station until he graduated to grease monkey and did oil changes and lube jobs and came home with most of the oil and lube on his face and shirt.

Plenty of limberdicks cruised the aisles at Ferguson's and eventually made their way through Nicole's line. The ones with a lick of sense in their otherwise brain dead thick skulls knew not to mess with her too much. Most of them knew she slugged a guy at Bunnie's Tavern one night for resting his hand on her thigh too close to her crotch while he tried to bullshit his way into her panties. She had swung for a homer and knocked the man right off his bar stool and he chipped a tooth when he hit the floor.

But there was someone who came through the line sometimes, a definite stoner, but cute and polite, which counted for a lot with Nicole. She wasn't against smoking a little weed herself from time to time — not too much, mind you — and she didn't hold that against him. He had very long blonde hair with just the right amount of wave in it — subtle and not curly, and it sort of made her think of Gregg Allman; but the guy's face was different than Allman's — more classically-chiseled, she thought. Not gorgeous, not pretty, but a little like the face on one of those Greek statues she'd seen and admired on a high school field trip to that museum in Chicago. A strong but accessible face. One you didn't easily forget.

The guy was quiet but friendly when he shyly ambled through her line, but also something else — wary. It was as though he was always aware of what was behind him, like maybe there could be something gaining on him. Nicole liked the mystery of it. Mystery was in short supply in Argus. The guy wasn't from Argus and she didn't know where exactly he hailed from, or what he did to make a buck, and she liked the excitement of that mystery, too. She didn't think he was the type to grope her in a bar. Sometimes — strictly on a sort of daydream/fantasy level, mind you — she thought that if he were to be sitting next to her in Bunnie's, and the conversation was comfortable and easygoing, she wouldn't squawk if he lightly touched her knee.

On this day he came into the store with another man, a taller, tanned man she had never seen before who seemed to be all angles. And where did he get that tan this time of year? Florida? She sensed a great gulf of some sort between them, but she didn't think the other man was something to worry about. Just a feeling, and her feelings were usually pretty reliable. This new guy was handsome enough, and lean — clean-cut with just a hint of roughness around the edges — but all in all she really thought she preferred the other one, her regular — well, semi-regular. You never quite knew when he would appear and he tended to stock up on groceries as though he didn't plan to get to town often.

The new man exuded something different. She watched him walk, how he didn't seem to drift as much as her semi-regular (time to get his name). She concluded that the new guy had seen a good slice of the world somehow and he had been changed a little by it — some of it good, some not so good. She really felt herself quite the psychologist in waiting.

The two men disappeared down an aisle and Nicole resolved that it was the day to get some answers. A name at the very least. It was mid-afternoon and slow, only one other register running. Make sure they end up in my line, she advised the other girl, Julie, and I'll owe you one.

Julie popped her bubble gum. "But what if he comes to me instead?"

"Then smile, put out your closed sign, and politely explain there's a register problem."

Julie made a face. "But my register works good."

"Just put up the sign and pretend. Then take a break. We're not busy."

"Mr. Ferguson won't like that."

"Mr. Ferguson isn't here this afternoon. I'm in charge."

"Is that guy your boyfriend?" Julie smirked and scratched a pimply cheek.

"No, he's not my boyfriend. It's a store security issue."

"He's a shoplifter?"

"No, he's not a shoplifter. Just never mind about that. Just trust me, Julie. I just need to find out who he is and what he's about. That's all. He's a stranger, from out of town."

"He comes in all the time."

"Still, we need to know who people are - right?"

"If you say so." Julie had already started thinking about her cigarette break with one of the cute stock boys.

Nicole put on her plastic, practiced smile and checked the next customer. Everything comes to those who wait, she reminded herself. She could be very patient.

5.

Raul

Raul knew the guy was lying, of course. Fine by him. Stoned or straight, he didn't much care. Live and let live and all that shit. Everyone has his or her own secret. But that line about being between jobs was horseshit. He figured Jesse for a small-time dealer probably. Or maybe even a big one. Hard to say. He had dynamite dope, a shit-kicking GTO, money and no visible means of support, and hid like a mole in the woods. Yeah, he was a serious dealer all right. Whatever. Whatever makes your chimes ring. It didn't make any difference to him. Not really. Maybe a little, but not enough to pop a gasket. He could always get off the train at the next station if he didn't like the direction. He was just a passenger. Raul exhaled and handed the joint back to Jesse. They had lumbered along past the dam and were finishing the loop around the lake to catch another road into Argus. The dreamy Sergeant Pepper had faded and Jesse put on Revolver for the last leg to town.

At the IGA they parked in a far corner of the lot, away from other cars to avoid dents and scratches. Jesse was careful with the car, Raul noted as he tried to recall the last time he was in Ferguson's and had to endure the inevitable welcome-home-warrior bullshit from Old Man Ferguson, who had lost fingers at Chosin Reservoir in Korea and seemed strangely to be awfully happy about it (he called Raul his "brother in arms"). Was it just last week? Might have been. Very fucking possible. He wasn't entirely sure. Then he remembered and was embarrassed to know: it was the day before. The weed made time seem almost irrelevant. He wondered if there was something extra in it, but concluded he felt too good to pursue the thought. If he felt good, how bad could it be?

They slowly tumbled out of the GTO in a cloud of marijuana smoke, shit-eating grins spreading across their faces.

"Just fucking hammered," Raul said. "That's some sweet product."

"I know my agriculture, I guess." Jesse chuckled.

"I think you do."

"I know a guy," Jesse said, shrugging his shoulders. "He's the herb expert."

"You're just a consumer, is that right?" Raul said.

"Something like that. So, do they smoke a lot of weed in Vietnam? Hard to get over there, man?"

The guy was good at changing a conversation, Raul noted. Had to be a trick of his trade. Fly under that fucking radar, so close to the ground you can almost smack it. He wondered just how much walking-around weed Jesse carried on him. Not so much, probably — don't carry more than you can easily get rid of in a hurry if necessary. That had been true in the Nam — don't carry anything you didn't need to stay alive. Raul was willing to bet Jesse's stash was buried somewhere so deep in the woods not even the squirrels could find it. Like a VC tunnel, or bunker.

"Weed's cheap in the Nam, Jesse. It's everywhere. Little kids sell it to you when you walk down the road. You can trade a Coca-Cola for some."

"No dealers?" Jesse frowned.

"Everybody's a dealer," Raul said. "Pretty democratic, ain't it?"

"Bad business," Jesse said. "That's socialism, man."

"That's the Nam, man."

Inside, the lights seemed very bright and oppressive and Raul adjusted slowly. He turned to his left a little, toward the registers, to see who was around. Out of the corner of his eye he noticed that Jesse had already stopped and coldly, quickly, calculated how many people were around, who they were, what they were doing, then moved off so as not to attract attention any longer than necessary. Don't stand in one place long enough for someone to get a bead on you. Apparently that was as true for pissant dope dealers as it was for grunts in the Nam. But Raul no longer inhabited the Nam, the Green, the Machine that was Green and Extra Mean. Every day it seemed to get just a little easier to accept that. It was slow, excruciatingly slow sometimes, but steady progress nonetheless.

There was a good-looking babe at one of the registers. Gorgeous long black hair. Pretty damn tall, too. Amazon Woman. But a real looker. Sort of resembled Cher. Raul noticed that she glanced briefly at him — a snapshot look seeking the essentials — but lingered as she gave Jesse the once-over with a subtle smile. He made a note of all that. Some history, maybe? Like back in the Green, you noted things that stood out. They might come back later to haunt you. He turned back to Jesse, who was already halfway down the first aisle, pushing a cart and scanning shelves precisely.

"Wait up, ace. You're losing me."

But Jesse didn't look back. He plucked cans and boxes from shelves and kept moving, his mouth shut, his eyes straight ahead and not lingering on a face and risking conversation.

"The guy's a trip alright," Raul said softy as he labored to catch up. He checked around the end of the aisle carefully so as not to be ambushed by Old Man Ferguson. He knew it would make its way back to his folks, and he was way too drilled to pretend to care.

He caught up to Jesse over by the meat section. Jesse was sifting through the various cuts — T-bone, sirloin, some thick filet mignon. Raul was still amazed at the abundance of good food in America. The steaks were very red, just cut, and they made Raul hungry.

"Hey, ace — you're hard to catch."

"I like to get in and out." Jesse didn't look up and continued to evaluate the cuts. "You interested in grilling some steaks? Back at the hacienda?"

Raul stared at the red meat still oozing blood. His mind sort of froze for a moment. It all struck him oddly. The blood seemed to pulsate and then he developed a fleeting thought that the blood was drops of red wine, and that notion suddenly spun out of control: the blood of dead Cong — the blood of Christ. Very strange. That weed's a motherfucker, alright. He felt dread, and heat flashed and tumbled like one of those 5.56 rounds throughout his body. The image of Christ slowly faded, but he felt a desire for space, to have room to move.

"We can cook them over an open fire, man." Jesse said. "Juicy steaks, cold beer. Breakfast of champions, man."

Raul looked around nervously. There weren't many people in the store, and he had avoided Old Man Ferguson so far, though luck had a way of running out. And Jesse might be a chore to explain to people.

But those steaks looked pretty good, blood of Christ or not. Why not, he concluded. A guy had to eat. He fished in a pocket for a twenty and handed it to Jesse, who seemed surprised.

"Here, man. I'll spring for the steaks, and beer, too. The least I can do for the dynamite product."

Jesse hesitated. "You sure? I've got money."

"Pick out some good ones. Good and juicy." Raul glanced around again. "Man, do you mind if I wait outside? The walls are kind of closing in a little."

Jesse studied Raul's face a couple seconds. "Sure. No problem. That's cool."

"Thanks, man. I just need some air."

"Here," Jesse said, digging the car keys out of his jacket. "Start that bad boy up and pull over by the door."

"Yeah, right." Raul stared at the keys, saw his hands tremble slightly, and wondered whether he could handle the GTO the way he felt. He headed up the aisle toward the door. He looked back once, but Jesse had moved on. That boy was cat-quick, really light on his feet. In the Nam he'd probably have been a tunnel rat.

When he reached the end of the aisle he saw that Amazon babe at her register. She sure had a funny look on her face as he passed by and lurched quickly through the big automatic doors. Outside, with the sun on him and space to breathe, he felt better quickly. He felt like a diver who'd held his breath as long as he could and had finally burst through the surface of the water to gulp air. His pulse finally slowed down. He realized his forehead was sweaty. He leaned against a row of shopping carts for a minute and let the sun bathe his face, then strolled toward the GTO, glancing instinctively across his shoulder several times. He noticed a police car parked across the street from the store, but the cop just seemed to be smoking a cigarette and Raul decided it was nothing at all.

6.

Art

Art Millage, the new Argus police chief, had seen that cherry red GTO around town. It sure was a piece of work. Big-ass motor. Glossy shine. Shiny chrome wheels. Raised letter Goodyear tires. It stood out like a sore thumb, but it sure was a beauty. He admired it, knew it could haul some serious ass, though not in his city limits, by God. No, sir. Out on the county roads, well that was different. That wasn't his concern. That was county sheriff business out there, unless someone cracked up and then he might get called out. He knew that GTO probably got opened up pretty good once it cleared town. He could picture it, almost hear the whine of that motor, smell the burnt rubber, and see the blue smoke. But in town, in his town, there was none of that, and his town was way too small for that GTO to just slip unnoticed into traffic. Hell, there wasn't any traffic. That GTO was a one-car parade whenever it rolled into town.

Art was parked in front of Fleener's Hardware, across from Ferguson's. He lit a cigarette and watched the man walk out of Ferguson's and lean against a row of carts for a minute, his head up and staring into the sun. Art instinctively looked up, too, to see if there was something up there. But it was just blue sky. The man seemed oblivious to the world for that minute, just staring into the sun with his eyes closed, before finally setting off for the GTO in the back of the lot. Art wondered what was going on inside his head. That might be some useful information to have. He had seen the man once before, at the VFW. Didn't know his name yet. But he would. If he was in some sort of cahoots with that other one, the blonde longhair who drove the GTO, then it was probably a good idea to know all the players. That was smart. That was essential. Know who everybody is, where they go, and what they do when they get there.

He exhaled gray smoke, looked ahead through the windshield, and saw the mayor strolling down the street toward him. He rolled down the passenger window and Hedges Sullivan leaned his meaty, red face in. He'd been drinking his lunch at the VFW. Art could smell it from clear across the car.

"Got some hardened criminals cornered, Arty?"

Sullivan was a prick and a blowhard, but Arthur had covered for his portly ass once when the mayor nearly got caught banging his secretary and so he stayed out of Art's way. Art tolerated "Arty" from him because he knew it was a lame but sincere attempt at building goodwill, and he wanted the mayor available and receptive if he ever needed to call in the debt.

"Cigarette break, mayor. Crime's kind of slow today."

"And that's just how we like it, Arty. Am I right?"

"Couldn't be righter, mayor. How's business at the VFW?"

"A brisk lunch trade, Arty. Corned beef and cabbage today. That packs them in."

"Might give that a try myself a little later." Art pointed at Raul across the street in the Ferguson's lot, slowly drifting toward the GTO. "You know that guy, mayor?"

Sullivan rose up and cupped a hand over his eyes.

"Yeah. That looks like Dom Cruikshank. Yeah — that's Dominick."

"Dominick."

"Just back from Vietnam, Arty. Good kid. Problem?"

Art mulled that over: a veteran. Vietnam. Fresh from it. They could be squirrelly.

"No problem, mayor. Just curious, that's all. Just curious. Still getting to know everybody."

Art had been police chief just a year after ten as a patrolman in Chicago. He was 38 and his time on Chicago streets had kept him in good shape, though the past year had put a couple pounds around his middle. Too much sitting, not enough doing. But when the Argus job had come open, he opted for the slower pace. The safer pace. A bullet had grazed his cheek one night in an alley on Chicago's South Side and he still had the scar, though it took a close look to see it. Sometimes he could still picture the gun's explosive muzzle flash, still feel the sudden, searing impact as the bullet kissed the cheek like a bee's sting and he lost his balance and toppled into bushes.

"Well, I'll stay out of your hair, Arty," Mayor Sullivan said. "Got some city business to attend to."

Art watched the mayor waddle away for a moment in his rear view mirror. He knew the city business was probably a nooner with his secretary back at his office. He smiled. That was a good chip to have. A get out of jail free card when he'd need the mayor to line up behind him on something. Something would come up. It always did.

He lit another cigarette and closed his eyes for a few minutes, just smoking and flicking ashes out the window. He smoked too much. Maybe he would quit. Or cut down some. It was a fine day to sit and smoke, though. Spring had

settled in. He watched as Cruikshank revved up the GTO
and pulled it into a space by the door to Ferguson's. So,
a Nam vet, fresh from his cage. They could be goofy. You
never quite knew what you'd get. It could go either way. Art
had seen some of them in South Side taverns in Chicago.
Tough monkeys. Unpredictable. Drunks. Stoners. But not
all. Some were very nice. He played basketball at the Y with
some Nam vets who might as well have been priests, so
impeccable were their manners. Others — disasters looking
for a place to become a crime scene. That was probably true
enough after any war, but more so, it seemed to him, with
this war. It wasn't a popular one. He'd seen the anti-war
demonstrations on TV. He never mentioned it to a soul,
but privately he didn't believe in the war, either. A bill of
damaged goods stuffed up America's ass by old LBJ, Art
figured. The fallout from it reached American streets in ways
far beyond demonstrations. He knew that one Nam vet
had been shot by police over in Gary, Indiana, because he
walked out his front door one night with a rifle and decided
he was back in Vietnam, walking point for his platoon. Jesus
Christ. Scary shit. Hard to imagine. Train a kid to seek and
destroy and then send him home without an off button.

After a while the blonde longhair came out of
Ferguson's pushing a cart full of groceries. He knew that
one's name: Jesse. Jesse Archer. He had been around, out by
the lake, a long time. His story wasn't hard to figure. Art was
still formulating a response to it, though. It was tricky stuff
balancing personal views and official ones. He had to be
very careful. There were lines that were easy to cross. Once
across them, things changed and action was mandatory.

But ever since what happened that night in Chicago,
Art had resolved not to go looking for trouble. Go with the
flow, some folks said. Maybe that was what he was doing,

going with the flow with this kid Jesse, who was selling weed out of his trailer. Art had known that for months. He did business out on the lake, though, not in Art's town. Art called him Jesse James to amuse himself. The kid had done a good job of keeping a low profile so far, like a good outlaw should.

Nobody knew it, but Art had smoked some weed. Got it from his brother up in Oak Park. Claimed he just wanted some to sample so as to be better equipped to deal with druggies. Know the world of the perpetrator. He didn't have visions or fits of hysteria. He had smoked a joint out on his back porch, screened from view by a tall fence, and watched sparrows tittering on utility lines. He'd never noticed just how delicate and finely-featured they were, how nimble they could be — how pleasant their songs were. Dope probably affected people differently, like anything else. Some folks liked booze, some smoked the wacky-backy. He just didn't see it was worth that much of a fuss.

But he wondered if all that meant he really couldn't be a cop anymore. He didn't think so. Doubts came and went. He took care of his town. People didn't have to wait for him to show up. Out there, the lake — that was country. He didn't run things out there. Was it about live and let live? Maybe it was. He just didn't know. He suspected and trusted that he would figure it out. Until then, he just kept tabs on Jesse James. That was a hoot. The kid, though, qualified as a sort of outlaw. Anyway, he always had the easy out. He could always say he had been sitting on it, waiting for the right time, if Jesse James became a problem. After all, the mayor would have to back him. A good card to have indeed.

Art watched and chuckled as Jesse James and his new buddy Mr. Cruikshank clumsily loaded the GTO.

They almost tipped the cart over once. Art wondered if he'd have to get a nickname for the other one, too. Frank James, perhaps. The James Brothers. The James Boys. The James Gang. Frank and Jesse. Where was Cole Younger? Funny stuff. Did that make him Pat Garrett? He thought a moment. No, Pat Garrett was the sheriff who killed Billy the Kid, so it was said. He made a mental note to stop at the library and look up the James Boys. He was hazy on how they got started. He suddenly wanted to know why they were such popular outlaws.

He glanced casually as the GTO lumbered slowly out of the lot and down the street toward the road out to the lake. He even waved gently as they motored by and he got a nervous smile in return from Jesse James. He always knew where to find him. Something to think about, he thought. Something to think about. He got out and walked down to the VFW and ate corned beef and cabbage. He thought it was very good.

7.

Nicole

She had just handed Mrs. Fleener $1.53 in change when the man — the new one — came up the canned vegetables aisle in a hurry and breezed through the automatic doors. Nicole didn't know what to make of it. He was practically an angular blur as he breezed by. She watched him pause outside, then lean against a row of carts, his head tilted back and absorbing the sun. Weird. What was he looking at? Why did he suddenly bolt? These were mysteries she felt qualified to solve, and solve them she figured she would. Just a matter of time.

Nicole looked around for the other one, her guy, but didn't see him. When she looked out the window again the new guy was gone and all she could see was that new police chief, Art Somebody, parked across the street in his squad car, smoking a cigarette.

The other cashier, Julie, had noticed the man leave, too, and shrugged, popping her gum as always.

"Where's your new boyfriend?" Julie said.

"Don't call him that."

"Why not? You're hot for him, aren't you?"

"How long do you want to live?" Nicole said and Julie got the message straight away and let the smirk fall apart on her face.

Nicole stepped out from her register and looked down an aisle, then another, and was relieved to see the other guy, her guy (why did she insist on calling him that?) pushing a full cart toward her. She composed herself and sauntered back to her register.

"Put your sign out, Julie."

Julie was ahead of her.

"I'm, like, already on break." Julie plucked a Benson and Hedges from her purse and skipped toward the loading dock, the unlit cigarette dangling from her mouth.

Nicole watched her guy push his cart around the corner of an aisle and pause, looking each way before slowly entering her lane. He pulled a jug of detergent from the cart and sat it on the conveyor belt, but Nicole purposely didn't engage the belt just to mess with him and see how he'd react. He piled up a few more items behind the detergent and dropped a pack of Oscar Meyer wieners on the floor before he realized nothing was moving.

"Don't hurt yourself," Nicole said as he rose up. She hoped it had sounded friendly, even seductive. She offered her best smile.

He had a deer-in-the-headlights stare, still clutching the pack of wieners. He shifted it from hand to hand and finally dumped it on the belt like it was a hot potato.

"Sorry," he said shyly. "I can go get another pack." He motioned toward the aisles, she noticed, as though he somehow thought she must be unfamiliar with the store.

"That's why we have baggers." She immediately worried she sounded too gruff. "Did the pack open?" She tried to sound sympathetic.

He picked it up and examined it as though there could be gold inside. He had an intensity about him. She was sure he was the type to analyze things. Like her.

"I don't think so," he said. "It's not leaking. But I'll be happy to go –"

"No," she said, and her voice seemed to startle him. "I mean, I'll have one sent up."

Nicole used the store speaker to call up one of the baggers. She noticed that the sound of it seemed to rattle him a little.

"Are you OK?" she said. Then she remembered he was probably stoned.

"It's loud. The speaker, I mean." He attempted a smile and for the most part pulled it off.

"It'll just be a minute," she said soothingly. "I hope you're not in a big hurry."

"Oh, no," he said, his eyebrows jumping a little. "Everything's cool. Really. I'm really sorry for being so clumsy."

His smile had blossomed. He was very polite, as always, and she liked that about him very much. She sensed — and hoped — he possessed a gentle soul.

"So, let's just work some of these other items through," she said. "While we're waiting." She cranked her smile up a notch.

"Right. Yeah — here, I'll just –"

"It's OK," she said. "Take your time."

He paused again, looked at her, even seemed to blush a little. He emptied the contents of the cart: steaks, a case of Pabst beer, packaged ham, a bottle of Boone's Farm, a bottle of Mateus, a bottle of Liebfraumilch, more wieners, mustard, bread, A-1 steak sauce, toilet paper, paper plates, plastic utensils, napkins, Birdseye frozen vegetables, baked potatoes, a dozen frozen dinners, orange juice, milk, canned asparagus, canned green beans, canned baked beans, chili con carne, Dinty Moore beef stew, canned soups, etc.

She rang items quickly. "Someone's having a picnic, it looks like."

"Picnic? No, not really. Well, sort of just a cookout. No big deal. Just steaks, potatoes." His voice trailed off and Nicole followed his gaze out the window, to the police chief sitting in his car across the street.

All she knew for sure and solid was that the Chief was new and from Chicago. She wasn't sure yet what his story might be. But she would be. Most everyone passed through her line sooner or later and revealed a bit of their life by what they bought. Her line was like a prime nexus for Argus. The Chief was nice-looking for an older guy — about forty, she guessed. Whenever he came through her line he was quiet, friendly enough, but didn't seem to invite small talk much. Once she noticed a subtle scar on his cheek and wondered what made it, what the story was behind it. Had to be a story. She was awfully sure she was good at ferreting out stuff like that. She was sure she'd figure it out.

"That's the new police chief," she said. "And the tubby guy leaning in the window, that's the mayor. Mayor Sullivan. Hedges Sullivan. It's sort of an unusual name — don't you think?"

Whenever Mayor Sullivan cruised through her line she could smell booze on his breath and he always teased her a little too freshly.

"Oh," was all Jesse said. But he kept glancing at the police car.

Nicole snapped her fingers and Jesse looked back at her with a grin. "Sorry."

"No problem. I was saying it's kind of an odd name."

"Yeah, it is. I guess I never heard anyone called that before."

Nicole had her opportunity and drove a truck through it.

"I'm Nicole Beckert." She extended her hand. Men liked to shake hands. She knew that. "So, what's your name?"

He was slow to take the hand. When he did she liked how warm his hand felt against hers. It wasn't a big old fleshy catcher's mitt and it wasn't too small or dainty, like a girl's, either. It seemed about right. No hairy knuckles, either.

"Jesse."

"Jesse James?" she said tartly, hoping to get a rise out of him.

"I get that a lot," he said. "Jesse Archer."

Finally, a name to go with the face. And the name seemed to fit him, too. She approved. He sort of was a little like an outlaw with that flowing hair, the stoner attitude, the mystery about where he might be from, what he did for a living. Maybe he even was some fugitive, like from Chicago, hiding out in Argus. If he was, though, she decided it wasn't because he was bad — misunderstood, probably. Yes, that could be it.

"So, Jesse," she said, lingering a bit on the syllables. "What's the occasion?"

"Occasion?"

"For the cookout."

"Oh. None, really. There's a guy I met — he was here in the store, but needed some air, and –"

"I saw him leave. Is he OK?"

"Oh, yeah. He just got back from Vietnam. I think he's still getting used to American ways again, if you catch my drift."

Vietnam, she thought. Wow. That explained a lot. She had that guy figured as having come from a long way out. And that explained the fading tan.

"He's an old friend?" she said.

"Nope." Jesse gazed out the window again, at the police car. The mayor had disappeared and the cop was looking over at the Ferguson's lot.

"You were telling me about your friend."

"Oh, yeah. Well, I just met Raul."

"Raul?"

"Yeah. That's what he goes by. His real name is Dominick. Dominick Cruikshank."

"Cruikshank?" The gears turned in Nicole's head. "I think there's a Cruikshank family here in Argus. I'm pretty sure I've heard the name. It stands out."

"That's him — his family, I mean," Jesse said. "He's from Argus. He picked Raul because it's shorter, easier."

Nicole frowned. She hadn't known who Raul was. But if he had gone into the army and then Vietnam, then she wouldn't have known him. Couldn't have. She would have been still a teenager. Therefore, it wasn't a case of a lapse in her powers of observation and information gathering. That made her feel a little better.

"It's an odd name for around here," Nicole said, still wondering a little whether she should have known about Raul, and why she didn't.

"Like Hedges."

"What?"

"Raul's different — like Hedges."

"Oh," she said. Snap out of it, Nicole, she told herself strenuously. "Sorry, I was thinking about something for a second."

She bagged the groceries — where did that bagger disappear to, she wondered — and together they sat the last bag in his cart.

"Where's your salad stuff?" she said. "Salad's good for you. You really need tomatoes, cucumber, lettuce — olives spice up a salad quite nicely."

"Uh, I guess I didn't think of it," Jesse said, looking like he had been scolded. "I've been meaning to eat more salads. For sure."

"You really should," she said. "So, how did you meet this Raul?"

"He's camping out near me, out at the lake."

"You live at the lake?" Nicole was impressed. The lake colony was nice. Large homes and everybody seemed to have a boat dock and a boat.

"Not on the lake," he said. "I have a trailer, in the woods near the lake. The west side, across the causeway."

A trailer, she thought, not sure what to make of that.

"Is it one of those big ones, a double-wide?"

He smirked. "No, it's not. Smaller. Comfortable, though. It's just me out there."

At least he seemed to be single, she thought. That was something, anyway. But a trailer? She decided not to be snooty about it. After all, she didn't come from money, either. She was particular, but not a snob.

"You're not from Argus, Jesse."

"Bloomington."

"Really? Did you go to ISU?" Now she was getting somewhere. She was on the trail and would find out just who Mr. Jesse really was.

"For a while. I dropped out — to experience life a while."

"What did you study, Jesse?" She liked saying and hearing his name.

"All sorts of things." He seemed to reflect on it a moment. "I thought about being a writer."

A writer? Wow. That impressed Nicole. Writers were very thoughtful. They analyzed the world and made really deep comments about it. They saw things other people didn't see. She knew that sometimes they went off into the woods for a long time to contemplate just about everything. That was probably what Jesse was doing. He was in his contemplative phase, out in the woods. She remembered Hemingway from high school English. He didn't even go to college. He lived life and then wrote great stories and books about it. They had read A Farewell to Arms. Jesse was a little like Hemingway. And she was sure he could write well.

"Are you going back to ISU sometime?"

He looked down at his feet. "Maybe. I don't know." He looked up and grinned. "I'm working on it."

"I might go there, too," she said, picturing them going to classes together.

He put his hands on the cart's handle. "Well, I suppose I should take off."

Nicole went for broke.

"I could bring salad stuff," she said. "If that's OK, I mean." Her smile was at full strength.

He seemed incapable of speech and just stared at her.

"To the cookout," she added. "You forgot salad stuff and I can bring it. Now that we're acquainted and all. I'll make it in a big bowl and cover it with plastic and keep it in the cooler until it's time. It'll be nice and fresh. What kind of salad dressing do you like?"

That deer-in-headlights look again. "Uh, Thousand Island, I guess."

She clapped her hands together. "I thought so. You look like a Thousand Island man. I could just tell. So, it's OK if I come?"

He nodded. "Yeah. Sure. I mean, of course. You're very welcome."

Nicole beamed. He'd said very welcome, not just welcome. That was a good sign.

Jesse drew a crude map to the trailer on a grocery sack.

"I'll be there," she said. "With bells on."

"What?"

"It's just a saying. Never mind. See you at five."

"Right. At five."

Nicole watched him go through the doors and then went to the window to watch him some more. Outside he paused a second and glanced over at the police car, then turned and escaped her line of vision.

8.

Jesse

"Did you see that?" Jesse said after they passed the police car. "He waved."

"For sure," Raul said. "I caught that."

Jesse was careful to keep it under the speed limit. He kept track of the police car in his rearview mirror, but it didn't budge. His palms were moist. After they turned onto the lake road he kept looking for the cop to appear, but nothing happened and he finally relaxed a little.

"That cop always waves and smiles when he sees me," Jesse said. "He trips me out."

"That's their job," Raul said absently.

"Yeah, but he seems to single me out."

"Maybe because he knows you deal weed." Raul studied a Rolling Stones eight-track cover.

Jesse glanced at Raul, who didn't look up. They rode several miles in silence.

"I deal a little."

Raul eased back in his seat. "I think you deal more than a little."

Jesse tapped his fingers on the steering wheel.

"All right. I do a little business. But just weed and hash. Sometimes, some speed. That's it. I stay away from the heavy stuff."

"And the GTO is sort of like your dealer Batmobile?"

"That's funny," Jesse said. "I really did buy it from my uncle. He got married and needed some cash. It wasn't that much, really."

"That's cool, Jesse. Just asking."

"You okay with it? The dealing?"

Jesse knew that some folks liked to toke a little weed, but somehow drew a moral line between that and dealing. But if people approved of the right of people to smoke it, how could they oppose the supplier? The American sociopolitical structure, a phrase he recalled from a class at ISU, was just plain weird. Like how politicians in Congress railed against legalizing dope, then went across the street, probably, to celebrate their moral stand by downing enough Scotch to poleax a horse. Ban it all or ban none of it. But he wasn't sure about that, really. He'd read about Prohibition. He knew what the effect of that was. Jesse was an entrepreneur, like a liquor storeowner. Weed was a product, like alcohol. Why did folks have trouble seeing that? He understood business well enough. Demand created markets. He supplied that demand. Sometimes he really did think of himself as sort of a farmer. A modern, crop-specific farmer.

"Jesse, I don't tell people how to live. Just make sure you tell them I'm an innocent bystander when they come for you."

Jesse digested that. "You think they will?"

"I hope not, man. But you never know."

"You're an Argus boy," Jesse said. "Who's that cop?"

"Don't really know him. All I know is he's new. He came from Chicago and his name is Art Millage. Tell me more about this babe — Nicole."

"She's coming to the cookout."

"So you said. Twice. Jesse, are you stoned all the time, man?"

"Sorry, dude. Lately I've been thinking I ought to cut it back."

"You know what they say," Raul said. "Too much of anything makes it boring — something like that."

"Too much of anything just means you have a lot of it," Jesse said, chuckling. "Look at it that way."

"That's pretty good. Pretty snappy alright. But I don't think it works that way, man. There are limits to everything."

Raul slid the Stones tape in and "Sympathy for the Devil" bored into them.

When the song was over, Jesse said, "Limits to everything?"

"Most things," Raul said after a moment.

"Sex?"

"Sure," Raul said. "I guess."

"Why? I mean, why have limits on sex or smoking weed?"

"I don't know. There just are."

"Did you learn that in Vietnam?"

"I learned plenty of things in Nam, Jesse. But limits wasn't one of them. There are no limits over there."

Jesse nodded, tried to envision Vietnam, a land beyond limits, but could not beyond palm trees and helicopters — the TV image he'd seen when he still had a TV.

"I think it's to maintain a structure — limits," Jesse said. "If everybody smoked weed all the time and fucked all the time, nothing would get done. But it would be fun."

"So true," Raul said. "But that line of thought could help put you out of business, man."

Jesse looked out his window at the cornfield. "I've been thinking about getting out of the business anyway."

"Then what?"

"I don't know." He recalled telling Nicole he wanted to be a writer. Where did that come from? Was it just bullshit? Could he even write? What would he write about? Dealing weed? Maybe. He'd done OK on the few college papers he'd done. "Did I mention Nicole's bringing salad? And Thousand Island dressing."

"You did. Several times."

"She's tall," Jesse said. "Kind of bossy, too."

"What do you think of her, Jesse?"

"I don't know. Women are hard to figure. She's pretty." Jesse hadn't had much luck with women in some time. Clarice, he knew, liked him well enough, but was drawn mostly like a moth to a flame because he had dynamite weed. She used to say it unlocked her creativity so she could be a better artist. Something like that. He thought that was bullshit. This Nicole was nothing like Clarice. Nicole seemed to have a strong will and knew what she wanted. She was brassy, ballsy. He wished he'd been a little less hammered so he could have talked seriously to her. What was serious, though? He wasn't sure. He figured it might be good to get straight awhile and go easy on the weed at the cookout. A cookout? It really was. He hadn't had company like this in a long time. Usually when people showed up it was just to do a deal, maybe try out the product first — hear a few tunes, drink a beer before the commerce got consummated. A stranger among strangers. This was different. He hoped.

"Well, she likes you, man," Raul said. "So I guess you got no choice but to figure it out."

"You think so?"

"She invited herself to your cookout. Earth to Jesse."

"Maybe she's just being friendly," Jesse said.

"Maybe that cop's just being friendly."

"Let's hope." Jesse instinctively looked in the rearview mirror, but saw nothing.

"You don't really believe that, do you?" Raul said.

"No," Jesse said. "Not a bit."

9.

Art

After his corned beef and cabbage lunch, Art cruised Argus. He did it daily so that he kept his finger on the town's pulse. It was a good little town, peaceful and safe, and he liked it quite well. He had a nice brick Tudor on a quiet street in a respected neighborhood sheltered by tall oaks. The house, he knew, would be an asset in attracting a wife, a notion he entertained lately more than in the past. A wife would be a social asset in Argus. So would a church. He would look for an acceptable church to join, one not too strict and judgmental. There was no real hurry and he even dreaded it some because a church was not a very comfortable place for him, even though it certainly would be reassuring to townspeople, to his neighbors. They would be pleased to see him sitting solemnly in a pew, even though Art preferred to have spiritual conversations alone, preferably outdoors with a lot of space.

The times Art had been in Chicago churches he had tended to daydream during the minister's sermon. He sometimes thought about the Bears or the Cubs, and often about startling things he saw as a street cop. But a church, he knew, would be fertile territory for finding a wife. Much more fruitful than the grocery store, though being in uniform at a grocery store had produced candidates in the past. Certain types of women were drawn to the uniform. He never fully understood it. It had something to do with the allure of authority. He knew that much. He had never married, though enough women had sailed in and out of his life like ships that apparently had other ports to visit.

Art cruised down his own street slowly. He lingered in front of his house a moment and grinned. He liked seeing the house from different angles. It presented very well indeed. If anyone saw him they would know he did that often and they might smile and shake their head approvingly. His neighbors valued his presence and he felt that many of them even liked him, too. Buying a solid house in a good neighborhood, instead of distant solitude in a farmhouse outside town, like the previous chief, stood him well right away with the townspeople. With good weather easing in, he would once again walk the neighborhood on some days just to say hello to whoever he ran into.

From Argus it was only about a hundred miles or so to Chicago, but it might as well have been a million miles away. Chicago had always seemed to him to be a twitchy gathering of tribes. It was a good enough place as cities went. Much better than New York City, which was ill-paced and too self-satisfied, and Los Angeles, which was too laid back and populated with narcissistic fools. He'd visited both those cities during his hitch in the Navy. His ship had supplied the troops in Korea and once he even got into Seoul for a few days. Compared with Chicago, Seoul had been chaotic and aromatic, but very interesting, and all in all Art had enjoyed trying to understand the South Koreans and their ways. Wherever he went, he tried to see that place through the eyes of the locals as much as being an American would allow.

Unlike Chicago, Argus was pretty much home to a single tribe that valued sameness, but was not necessarily a closed society like it could be sometimes in certain Chicago neighborhoods. Argus could be warm enough to strangers after a sort of probation period. Argus was close enough to ISU that some of it professors and other university types had drifted over to make it their bedroom community. Several professors lived in his neighborhood and he enjoyed the occasional lively political debate with them on the sidewalk or at Cameron's Café downtown. One just had to establish oneself and prove their worth. It had something to do with being surrounded by corn and soybeans and not existing in the gray shadows of skyscrapers. Expectations were different. Etiquette was more evident. People in Argus had more space, more breathing room than in Chicago and as a result personal space and breathing room were respected.

Art liked being chief of police. He did not consider himself to be intrusive beyond what the job required. When personal matters were involved, he tied to be discrete, even delicate. He understood a little about human fallibility. The Navy and Korea had taught him a little about that. He held a good marker on the mayor, but that was just prudent job politics. It wasn't personal. It was political commerce. Despite knowing Hedges Sullivan was a dickhead of sorts, Art nonetheless knew he was a well-meaning mayor and that he could work with him and understood that Sullivan was ruled mostly by his dick and booze. Art didn't feel qualified to sit in high judgment of the man. That was for a higher power — for God, or whoever it was pulling the strings. Someone with a lot bigger shoulders than his. We all had a lot to answer for later. It was a good thing to remember. He tried hard to remember it whenever he set foot in a church.

After leaving his neighborhood behind, it didn't take long to navigate the rest of town. There were still some hours of light left and Art wheeled by Cameron's for a coffee to-go and then called one of his officers by radio to let him know he was "going off the board" for a while. It was well understood that going off the board meant personal time, but he would be available by radio if something happened. Chief's prerogative. The privilege of rank, though Art would never abuse the privilege. He had three officers and had judged them all to be decent men and reliable enough to have the town left in their hands sometimes.

The day was so nice he decided to make a trip out to the lake. He enjoyed seeing the lake houses with their seawalls and docks and piers and sailboats with yellow and blue sails dotting the water like flocks of giant butterflies. It was still early in the season to see much on the lake, but he knew there would be a few fishermen in their jon boats working the bays out of the wind to fish for crappie and large mouth. He had lately daydreamed about buying out at the lake in a few years, when he had more equity in his house. He liked his house very much and knew he could live in it a long time. But down the road, say three or four years, he would be solid enough in town that a move out to the lake would not only be permissible, but a matter of course for someone moving up in the world. Art had received an injury settlement from his shooting in Chicago and had invested it in mutual funds. In a few years, he reckoned he could afford to sell and move out to the lake if it still appealed to him. The lake would be a fine place for retirement, though he figured that was twenty years off, when he'd have a nice Argus pension to go with what he had from Chicago. In retirement he would learn to fish and sit on his porch overlooking the lake, with a wife, of course, perhaps sipping a beer or even margaritas, and watch the sun set.

He drove slowly into the lake colony. There were really two distinct parts. The first was a section of nice homes that even Art would be able to afford. These people often told him how much they appreciated seeing his car, even though it wasn't his jurisdiction. Beyond that section, separated by thick woods, was a peninsula and the homes there were often quite large and expensive. Doctors and lawyers and such. Art would not be able to buy there without striking it lucky somehow. Some of those homes could truly be called mansions, at least by rural Midwest standards, and the president of ISU had recently bought there. Art had chatted with him one Saturday morning at Cameron's and found the man to be quite down-to-earth.

After a while Art said goodbye to the orderliness of the lake colony and drove to the other end of the lake. That end remained wild and undeveloped, a few farms lingering with the past when all of the lake had been farmland and trees before flooding made it a lake and gave affluent people a reason to covet it, and a few wise farmers the sense to profit by it. There was a county road that came up from the dam at the wild end of the lake, and Art knew there was a little rise just before the road joined the causeway where he could see the stand of woods that sheltered the tiny trailer.

Jesse James' trailer.

It was worth a look since he was already there.

10.

Nicole

She happily made a big wooden bowl of salad: cucumbers, tomatoes, celery, romaine and iceberg lettuce, salad peppers, a sprinkling of artichokes and grated cheeses, and olives, of course — green as well as black, and then she covered it with plastic and set off in her gray VW bug. She had made some deviled eggs, too, just in case the salad wasn't a hit. Men could be funny about salads. But she knew they liked deviled eggs a lot. She knew a lot of things.

She knew Jesse was from Bloomington (not a hick).

She knew Jesse had gone to college (potential).

She knew he might be a writer (more potential and thoughtful, too).

She knew he was polite, soft-spoken (compatible).

She knew he smoked weed, but that was OK (adventurous).

She knew he had a soft, warm handshake (dreamy, sensuous).

After she crossed the causeway, she missed the turn to Jesse's lane and had to go down the county road to the T to turn around. Before her turn she saw the police chief's car slip round the corner and for a second she made eye contact with the Chief, who waved and continued on slowly past her, then past Jesse's trailer, then across the causeway until his police car disappeared behind trees on the other side.

She knew that was odd.

11.

Jesse

He had looked up and there was that cop again, rolling slowly past the entrance to his lane. Jesse had just stepped out of the trailer with matches to light kindling for the fire. There could be no mistaking that the cop meant to be seen. His car practically crawled by and Jesse saw the bastard wave.

"He's out of his pond," Raul said. "Might be nothing."

"Yeah, but he's still a cop."

Raul had just come back from pissing behind a tree.

"Could be he's just sightseeing," Raul said. "He has a life, like everybody else."

"Could be," Jesse said. "Could be frogs can fly, too."

Jesse watched the cop cross the causeway very slowly until he disappeared behind trees on the other side.

"Think he's coming back?" Jesse turned to Raul, who still looked across the causeway.

"No. He's had his look. That was just recon."

"Recon?"

"Recon, man. A looksee. Checking the target. Getting the lay of the land."

"That's very reassuring," Jesse said.

"Best I can do," Raul said. "So, are you wired tight around here, Jesse?"

"What do you mean?"

"I mean your stash, bro. Your pot of gold and all that."

"Oh." Jesse thought of the place in the woods. "Yeah, that's taken care of. There ain't anything in the trailer. Just what I carry. I'm cool."

Raul surveyed the woods beyond the trailer. "Out there somewhere, right?"

"Maybe," Jesse said. He reminded himself that Raul had the potential to become a friend, but was still on probation. He had to be careful. Being careful had stood him well so far.

"Where else could it be, man?" Raul shook his head. "In a safety deposit box at the bank, for Christ's sake? Might be a man could walk out there and look for a worn path."

Jesse grinned, even felt a little smug.

"I thought of that. I always go at it from different directions. I don't trample plants. I walk like an Indian, man. Light, careful. Not even the squirrels could find it."

Raul nodded. "Groovy. Very damn groovy. Might make a soldier out of you yet, troop."

"No thanks. I'm not cut out to be a grunt." He had the same old fleeting thought about his low lottery number, but the thought didn't stick.

"Everybody's cut out to be a grunt, Jesse. They just don't know it until they're put in the bush with a weapon and a reason to use it."

Jesse wasn't sure what that meant. He knew Raul was still adjusting to being home. Back in the grocery store he seemed to even lose it a little. He had a habit of pissing outside all the time. Must not be used to indoor plumbing again yet, Jesse concluded. He liked Raul, but still had to be wary until he really knew what the guy was all about.

"I reckon," Jesse said. "Troop."

"That's it. You're catching the lingo, man."

The sound of a whiny engine turned them back toward the road and they saw the VW bug turn onto the lane. It hesitated for a few seconds before creeping onto the lane.

"Now who the fuck is this?" Jesse said. He didn't have any business scheduled. Not for today, anyway. There was that other thing, the big thing, but that was still fluid. It was still forming. He would yet need to go to town and use a phone and make arrangements. This wasn't about that, and he knew it couldn't be a cop, not in a VW bug. Unless it was a narc. Could be a narc, but Jesse had never heard of any around there. Over in Bloomington-Normal, sure. But not in the boonies. He was pretty sure on that. He had talked to people. People who knew about those things. He watched the VW slowly, cautiously navigate the lane toward them and he could finally make out long hair on the driver's shoulders.

"It's Amazon Woman," Raul said. "Your date's here, man."

12.

Art

He had been tempted to go back, just to throw another curve at Jesse James. He'd even abruptly turned around in a farmer's lane and crept the car to the edge of the trees sheltering the road from the lake. But there was really no sense in spooking him any more than he just had. If he went back, it would be too much. He had a good sense of those things. As it was, Mr. James would have to debate whether it was just coincidental or a shot across his bow. He'd have to entertain the possibility it was just a joyride on a nice damn day around the lake. But there would always be doubt. Let him chew on that a while. It might even motivate him to remember the boundaries. Boundaries were important. Art was doing his job and containing the situation, he decided. This Jesse James issue was not black and white to him. For the moment he felt that keeping the business out of his town was duty enough. He knew what he felt good about and what he felt bad about, and this felt right enough.

That girl, the one who checked groceries at the store, looked pretty surprised to see him. She had quite the quizzical look on her face as he slipped by her. He had waved and smiled to make it seem routine. Just a drive in the country on a superb day. She was one of his people, after all. In his rearview mirror he saw her go up the lane to the trailer. So, she was a player, too. Maybe. Maybe not. He'd get to the bottom of that, too. She might just be someone's love interest. That wasn't any of his business. He respected those things. He wanted the same respect in those matters. But if she was someone's girl, he wondered which one it was? Jesse James? Or Mr. Cruikshank — Mr. Crankshaft, he'd started calling him for amusement. Would she go for the dreamy blonde outlaw or the hardened veteran? Either way, she would certainly reinforce his presence to Mr. James and so it was very helpful she saw him. Could be she was a customer. That was fine. Whatever. People made choices. You couldn't decide for them all the time. He'd find out eventually. That was certain.

But Art didn't think the girl came across as involved in drugs. He could be wrong, of course. Being a cop meant understanding that appearances could easily deceive. His cop's gut, though, signaled she was on the up and up for the most part. Just a feeling. Whenever he passed through her line at Ferguson's she was friendly and sort of commanding. She seemed like a tough girl without coming across as harsh, one who didn't take much crap from any dickhead who might come along and make a dumbass joke about bananas as she checked them through. Men would naturally be drawn to her beauty, that long dark hair, but they would be intimidated by her, too.

Someone at the VFW told him the one about how she decked a guy at Bunnie's Tavern when he tried to play house with her thigh. She was a tall girl. He could imagine it. Art would have liked to see her do it. He wouldn't have arrested the man, figuring he got what he deserved and punishment had been meted out. There was an air about her. Independent — that was the word he was searching for.

This girl, Nicole, came across as independent. Sure, maybe she smoked a little weed here and there. These days, who didn't? He was very clear with himself on how he felt about that. He wondered what people would think if they knew just how many so-called solid citizen of Argus smoked a little in the privacy of their own homes, yet maintained the outward hypocrisy that it was evil somehow. He still had some at home. He had been meaning to try it a second time just to see if it made a difference. What would people think if they knew he smoked it? They wouldn't find out, number one. He was very careful. Two, he would use the line about knowing a perpetrator's world. The mayor would have to back him on that.

Art drove back into town and checked in, then went home. On the way he nearly stopped at Ferguson's to see if somehow Nicole was back at work. It would be funny to go through her line again so soon. It might reveal something useful. Instead, he went on home. He had groceries. There was plenty of time to run into her and see what developed. If she was older, say, ten years older, he might wonder about her as a potential girlfriend. But those ten years were likely as good as fifty in some ways. She was maybe 21 and he pushed forty. She checked groceries and he'd been to war. Well, near one, on a ship — the war had been there, somewhere in the distance, beyond impassive coastal mountains, and once he heard big guns booming and saw jets attack a target he could not see. He shared war with Mr. Crankshaft, he noted. And he had been shot. Not badly, but shot. How many people could say that? She was just two years or so out of high school. Different worlds altogether.

At home in his bright kitchen he made a cheeseburger and ate some leftover potato salad with it. He tried to watch TV a while, but Walter Cronkite was a little too sobering in his report from Vietnam. Art watched men running to and from helicopters on the screen, the big rotors flattening the tall grass around the landing zones. He thought of Korea, his war, for a few minutes. His ship had been as safe off the Korean coast as if it was anchored in San Diego or Hawaii. He had visited both of those ports and remembered the palm trees and gorgeous weather fondly. But California really wasn't a place for Midwesterners. Not for very long, at least. Californians expected things to always be easy. Midwesterners knew what it meant to struggle and work for something. He felt there was a profound difference between the two regions. One had all the weather and no sense, and the other was more grounded in reality and understood the changing weather to be just part of life's challenges. He accepted California with a large grain of salt, though San Francisco was a port he had somehow missed and he regretted it. He though that city would have been a treat to visit. He really had seen some of the world and understood it to a degree and that pleased him. It made staying in one place that much easier.

After he turned off the TV, he wandered through his house. It was a fine place and truly felt like a home, though it could get lonely sometimes. So he made plans to try one of the churches, the Presbyterian one, on Sunday to see if there were any eligible ladies. If there were, he would almost certainly be introduced by some eager citizen who wanted to curry favor — or maybe just wanted to see him happy. He knew a few women from the VFW, or Bunnie's Tavern, but places like that could be dicey. It was OK for getting laid, but often the women there might have a drinking problem, or be married and looking to screw around behind a husband's back, which was a dangerous practice in a town as small and tightly connected as Argus.

Later he went out on the back porch in the dark with the small baggie of dope and filled the pipe bowl. He could not get the hang of rolling a joint between thumbs and forefingers. His efforts always produced something tattered and too loose. The pipe made it easier and worked just fine. He smoked a full bowl slowly, remembering to hold the smoke in as long as he could. He laughed out loud, figuring Jesse James might be doing the very same thing out there on the lake.

13.

Nicole

The campfire had settled down to glowing embers and Nicole was pleased that Jesse had fetched her a lawn chair and a glass of cold Liebfraumilch and in general fussed quite nicely to make her feel comfortable and welcome. At first, though, he had seemed pre-occupied and even a little agitated with the chief of police's appearance.

"Well, he's gone now," Nicole said, trying to change the subject. She was eager to hear about Jesse and his desire to be a writer. That was exciting.

"It's just weird, that's all," Jesse said. "I was just surprised. Cops have a way of finding something wrong, no matter how hard you try to follow the rules."

"Following those rules pretty closely, are you, Jesse?" Raul smirked.

"You know what I mean," Jesse said.

"You're used to running wild and free, is that it?" Nicole said. She was trying to be funny. She thought that Jesse got that. She wasn't sure what Raul meant. The tone made her curious.

Jesse shrugged. "Yeah, something like that. It's cool. It just threw me off for a while."

"Well, it doesn't have to be a downer," she said. "Right?"

Jesse brightened "No. Not at all. I'm glad you came."

"Me, too," she said, and briefly they clasped hands.

"Jesse's got his shit wired, so no biggie," Raul said, lagging behind in the conversation.

Nicole wondered just what that meant, too. She caught the look, though, that Jesse shot Raul. She knew Jesse had weed. All that stuff about the cop was just a little paranoia, she figured. It was kind of cute, really, how his face got such an intense look to it. It made him seem older, analytical. Writers had to be serious sometimes because they wrote serious things. She acknowledged it was a little odd to see the Chief so far out of town. This was the boonies. What was he doing out on the lake? She hadn't been far behind him when he slowed nearly to a stop for a moment at the lane to Jesse's trailer. She remembered that he had been parked in front of the store, too, when Jesse and Raul were there. It did have a funny feel to it. But she figured the Chief was new to town and still seeing everything. And a dilapidated trailer in the woods did sort of catch a person's eye when they drove by.

"People just naturally gawk at things out in the country," Nicole said. "So, do you have any music? You can't have a cookout without music."

"Whatever you want," Jesse said. "I've got music out the wazoo."

Raul volunteered and put on some Jefferson Airplane and the three of them pulled their chairs closer to the fire against the coming evening chill. Jesse slapped the steaks on a grill secured over the embers. Nicole liked the sound of the sizzling steaks and she noticed that Jesse did, too. Raul sat slightly apart from them, signaling, she estimated, his acknowledgment of her interest in Jesse. But he was friendly enough, too, despite the subtle dark aspect that trailed him, and he had talked to her about growing up in Argus and told funny stories while Jesse gathered dinner. She and Raul had endured many of the same teachers at Argus High.

Jesse had wrapped potatoes in foil and wedged them on the edges of the fire to cook slowly. Everything smelled good. With a wide grin, Jesse lit a joint and passed it around. Nicole had expected that. She grinned back at him. He was very shy about making eye contact with her but did his best. She was sure he liked her. It was strange but very exciting to be in such a romantic atmosphere and to get to know him after all the brief encounters at Ferguson's. She only took a few hits. She was careful about it. She enjoyed a good light buzz, but she liked to keep her wits about her. Jesse was very understanding. He didn't try to talk her into doing more, like so many boys did at parties in high school. He seemed to know people had limits and respected them.

"Tell me about your writing, Jesse." The music had been changed to The Moody Blues' In Search of the Lost Chord, and everything had slowed down. She felt mellow.

"Writing?" He poked the fire with a stick and sparks rose up into the blackness. He watched them a moment.

"You said you wanted to be a writer."

"I guess I did. I don't know. Something I thought about at ISU."

"What did you major in at ISU?"

"I just took classes, really. Picked what sounded good." He poked at the fire some more with the stick. "I guess you'd say I was majoring in life."

"Deep," Raul said. "Very deep, man."

Nicole leaned forward in her chair. "It is deep," she said. "A good writer must experience life."

"You learned that in school," Raul said. "Things get a little different once you're out."

"You learned that in Vietnam," Nicole said. He definitely had his dark side.

"I reckon I did," he said, looking away and into the fire. "Things got a little different after school, didn't they Jesse?"

"A little," Jesse said. "Just a tad."

"You guys have some secret code going on here," Nicole said. "So, cut it out." But she tacked a smile on to let them know she wasn't entirely serious. "Tell me what you've written, Jesse."

"Jesse's been writing about markets, Nicole," Raul said. "Products and markets and sales. He's sort of a business writer."

"Yeah," Jesse said. "That's so true."

But she could tell Jesse lacked sincerity. Raul had said it good-naturedly, and while Jesse seemed to take it well enough, there was definitely a submerged issue there.

"Good writers can write about anything," she said, trying to be encouraging. "Good writing can make anything seem interesting — even business."

"His business is pretty interesting alright," Raul said, but there wasn't much edge to it anymore and Nicole wondered whether he might even have felt he talked out of turn and regretted it.

"She's right, man. Good writing is good writing." Raul raised his can of PBR. "How about a toast?"

Nicole and Jesse raised their wine glasses. "What do we toast?" Jesse said.

"To better times than these," Raul said. "To the future."

"And writers," Nicole added.

"Sure," Raul said. "To writers."

"Why not," Jesse said. "To my first book, whatever that is."

"There you go," Nicole said. "It could happen."

Raul finished his beer and stood up. "Is the couch still mine, Jesse?"

"It is, man. All yours, commander."

"Then that's where I'm headed. It's been a long day. Good night, Nicole."

"Sleep tight," she said.

"And watch out for the bedbugs, right?"

"That's right."

Raul patted Jesse on the shoulder. "Bro, I think I'm hammered. Sorry if said anything weird."

"No sweat," Jesse said. "Just take a blanket off my bed. And there's an extra pillow, too."

"Thanks, man. Beats the ground."

After Raul went into the trailer Jesse filled their glasses and gave Nicole a sweater to slip on and they walked down the lane to the lakeshore. The moon was almost full and the lake was calm. Jesse kissed her, a long, wet kiss, and then he slipped his arm around her waist and she placed her hand over his and they walked the lakeshore for a while like that. Jesse told her everything. He told how he met Raul and how he flunked out of college. He told her he dealt weed, too. You know, he had said, here and there. There and here. She wasn't particularly surprised and she wasn't really disappointed either, she claimed. Not really, though there had to be limits. Limits could be healthy and life-reinforcing. Everybody smoked weed and it had to come from somewhere. But she had always felt it wasn't how a person started. It was how they finished.

"It takes an awful lot of things to make the world go around, Jesse."

"I'm not a writer, Nicole. That was just bullshit. Stoned bullshit. But maybe I could be. I don't know."

"Just be yourself," she said. "That's a start."

"Things do have to change," he said. "I do need a new start."

"Are you still worried about that cop, the chief?"

"Maybe. Maybe he's a sign of some kind. I can't get it off my mind. I can't shake the feeling he knows what's going on."

"Could be," she said. "But if he does and wanted to do something about it, why hasn't he?"

"I don't know. Maybe he's like a cat playing with a mouse before the kill."

Nicole laughed softly.

"That's funny?"

"No. But it was cute. I wasn't laughing at that. My dad used to say that if you didn't want to get run over, don't stand on the road. And if you want to get somewhere, look both ways before you cross."

"Deep," Jesse said.

"Very. Now, kiss me again because I have to go home."

"Do you really have to go?"

"Yes. You live in a messy trailer with a roommate and this is our first date. I don't sleep over on first dates."

"What about the second?"

"That's negotiable."

14.

Raul

He got up before the sun had a chance to peek over the horizon. Too much beer and weed from last night. Raul poured a glass of orange juice and sat on the couch a while to wake up as it got lighter. He looked in on Jesse, who appeared to be down for the count a while. Maybe he was dreaming of sugarplum fairies and his new girlfriend. She was a good one, that Nicole. Sassy and strong and opinionated. He figured to find one just like her if he could. But there was plenty of time for that. That would work itself out. It always did.

There was a campground about a quarter of a mile west of the trailer along the Kelton Road that had bathrooms and a coin-operated shower. He didn't think anyone would be camped there yet and he got dressed and located his duffel with the last clean clothes and borrowed a towel, soap, and one of Jesse's Chicago Bears sweatshirts. The shower was warm and he stood under it a long time. He scrubbed himself thoroughly and brushed his teeth and the clean clothes made him feel positively human again.

He was very hungry and wanted one of those big Midwestern breakfasts. There was a small country café at an intersection halfway up the road to Argus. That was about three miles. He pondered it a moment, then decided to hoof it up there. The exercise would help clean his body and clear his mind. Both needed it. He stopped at the trailer and rummaged in Jesse's fridge and found some packaged ham. He opened it and folded several slices and filled the middle with mustard to stave off hunger for a while. He wrote a note for Jesse and left it on the counter. He guessed they must be friends now if he was leaving a note. He wondered how Jesse would view that. He'd been a little rough on the boy last night. Said some things that were prickly. He was out of line and figured to square it later.

By time he'd crossed the causeway, he had a good marching rhythm going. Humping was humping and the Army made you good at it sooner or later. The birds were happy in the trees along the road and the sun was bold and orange. He did the old Army trick of not thinking as he humped, just focusing on arms and legs and moving and just being an element among other elements. When he looked up, the café was there on his left. A smattering of trucks and cars dotted the lot. A semi-tractor was pulling in with an empty car trailer behind it. Inside, the smell of cooking sausage and bacon filled the air and he found a stool at the counter near a window where he could watch the sun climbing. Only a few people were eating breakfast yet. The clanking of silverware and the hissing of eggs on the grill were reassuring to him as he sipped his coffee.

Raul ate scrambled eggs with bacon and sausage links and toast and hashed browns. He smiled as he ate, thinking Jesse would call it a breakfast of champions. The waitress topped off his coffee and took his plate when he was done eating and he impulsively ordered a slice of apple pie with whipped cream on top. After the pie, he swiveled on his stool to let the sun blaring through the window scrub his face. He sat that way for several minutes until he heard someone slide onto the stool next to him. He opened his eyes and there was the chief, Art Millage.

"Good morning, Mr. Cruikshank," Art said. "You don't mind if I join you, do you?"

Raul wasn't surprised the Chief knew his name. That was his business. And Raul was well-known at the VFW, where he knew the Chief liked to go, too.

"Not at all, Chief."

"Call me Art, if you like." He hailed the waitress for coffee and a menu. "I confess that I'm still so new around here I still look at the menu. What did you have?"

The Chief was pretty good, Raul thought. Good at small talk but controlling the dialogue, getting information.

"Scrambled eggs, bacon, links, toast — breakfast of champions, Art."

"Sounds like it." Art studied the menu intently. "I'm pretty hungry myself."

Raul wondered whether this was coincidence or not. The Chief might have chosen Cameron's in town for breakfast. It was sort of the Argus hub and smack across the street from his office. This country place was mostly farmers and a few lake people on their way to jobs in Bloomington-Normal. But it was known for its breakfasts and maybe that was all there was to it. Random shit. The universe could be pretty fucking random alright. Either way, it was no big deal to Raul. He didn't have anything to hide, nothing to fear the Chief about. If the Chief turned out to be a tough guy, so be it. He'd seen a lot tougher in the Nam.

"Have you tried the spicy potatoes, Mr. Cruikshank? Pretty damn good. I had some last week."

"That's what I hear," Raul said. "Been a while since I had them. I haven't been in here in years." He needed to do something about the Mr. Cruikshank crap. In high school, kids even tried to call him Mr. Crankshaft.

"That's right," Art said without looking up. He was leaning over his steaming plate and smelling the potatoes. "You're just back from Vietnam. Pretty rough was it?"

Raul thought a moment. "I'm still in one piece."

"I can see that," Art said. He took a bite of potatoes. "These potatoes are amazing. I wonder what they put on them. I keep trying to figure that out. I guess I should just ask."

"That's how you find things out alright," Raul said. "Call me Dom if you like."

"Short for Dominick," Art said.

"That's right." Raul wasn't sure whether to unleash Raul on the Chief. He wondered if the Chief wasn't one of those who would find it odd and let it somehow get in the way. And maybe Raul wasn't operative as much as before. It was what he'd picked up after high school, when he enlisted and didn't know his ass from a hole in the ground. That was a fucking long time ago. Another world, another time.

"You were saying about Vietnam," Art said.

The guy's persistent, Raul thought. The kind of guy who keeps boring in when he needs to know something.

"Actually, I wasn't." Raul figured to test the Chief out a little.

Art nodded, smiled. He scooped up some potatoes with his fork. "Fair enough. It was Korea for me. Navy."

"That a fact?" Raul was mildly surprised. He'd figured the Chief was a career cop who'd probably skated when it came to military service. "That's interesting — Art."

"Oh, probably not as interesting as yours." Art called for more coffee and complimented the waitress on the potatoes. "I was on a supply ship. We spent our tour off the coast. I got into Seoul once and saw the sights. Pretty low-key, really. Nothing like your war. Heard some stuff blow up a couple times. Kind of abstract, really."

"I see." Raul was calculating what the Chief thought his war was like. At least the man didn't try to puff up his own experience. That was in his favor.

"But I didn't mean to bring up anything rough, though," Art said. "Vietnam's a different war. Just watching it on TV, you can tell that."

"Yeah," Raul said. "For sure." He really was good. Of course you meant to be rough if it helps open someone up. That's what you do.

Art covered his cup when the waitress offered more coffee. "Thanks, but no. Too much caffeine and all that."

Raul got up to go. "Well, Chief, got to shove off. Nice chatting with you."

"I'll walk out with you. I want to ask you something."

Of course, Raul thought. Soften up the target before going in.

Outside, it had become a gorgeous day and Art mentioned it while Raul waited for the small talk to get shoved aside.

"Did you walk up here, Dom?"

"I did. Needed to stretch my legs."

"I hear you on that. I need to get some exercise myself. Cops sit too much."

"What can I do for you, Chief?"

"That's perceptive of you, Dom. Well, it's not so much what you can do for me, though there's some of that, too. It's what you can do for Jesse Archer. He's a good friend of yours?"

A good question, Raul thought. The answer was more yes than no.

"Chief, I just met the guy. I'm camping out his way and he invited me to hang out and drink a couple beers. Good neighbor stuff. Not much of a story."

"That's fine," Art said. "Nothing wrong with that. But we both know he's a bit of an entrepreneur, if you get my meaning."

"Entrepreneur?" Raul fumbled for a cigarette and lit it. "You mean like in real estate? Something like that?" Another fastball for the Chief, he thought, and let's see how he swings at it.

Art chuckled. "I'm glad your sense of humor's intact. That's pretty important. Some guys come back from war without it. That's pretty funny about real estate. You must have kept them in stitches over in Vietnam, Dominick."

"Dom's just fine."

"So let me be straight here. Dom. You don't know Jesse's business?"

Raul shrugged. "He's got cold PBR in the fridge. And the couch ain't too bad for sleeping." He looked off at the sun and had to cup his eyes.

"And that's all you know," Art said. "Have I got that right, Dom?"

Raul took a drag on his cigarette and exhaled slowly.

"Jesse said he went to ISU awhile, but now he doesn't. Said he had some money saved from some job. He lives cheap, Chief, I can honestly say I ain't seen any business going on out there, real estate, diamonds, or otherwise. Ain't seen anybody but Jesse and the inside of his fridge."

"And that girl from town. Nicole."

Raul nodded. "She did drop by last night. That's right. You popped by, too."

"I didn't make a secret of it, son."

"No, you didn't," Raul said, noting the strategic use of the word son. The Chief didn't have as much war as Raul, so he was trying to assert wisdom and experience through age. "You rolled by slow enough to take a picture, chief."

"Maybe I did. Ok, Dom, I see where you're coming from."

"You do, Chief?"

"I don't think you're part of Jesse's deal. But you're standing awful close to it."

"Close only counts in horse shoes and hand grenades, Chief." Raul wasn't afraid of the Chief. He didn't have shit on him and Raul didn't come all the way back from Vietnam to get a shake down from some torque-up badge that spent his war on a cozy ship gulping ice cream and counting toilet paper rolls.

Art grinned. "You've got a million of them, don't you?"

"I was a boy scout, Chief. Be prepared and all that."

"Well, that's fine. I'm happy for you, Dom. Let's hope Jesse doesn't become a grenade and you aren't standing close when he goes off."

That was plain enough. Raul figured the dance was over.

"So, Chief, did you come out all this way just to see me?"

"Nope. Not at all. I came out for the potatoes, swear to God. And they were excellent as always. But when I saw you I took the opportunity. That's my job."

"What are you telling me, Chief?"

Art looked at the ground a moment, then off at the trees covering the lake from view. "I guess I'm telling you that as long as Jesse stays on the lake and does his thing out there, I don't much care. But he can't ever bring it to town. And if I hear about any problems associated with it, even out at the lake and away from my town, the equation changes. It would have to change. Fair warning. That's all this is."

"OK, Chief. Good enough. I'll mention to him that the real estate market in town is all full up."

Art grinned. "You're a corker, Dom."

"So they say." But Raul was curious about the Chief's live and let live attitude. Where did that come from? Must be something behind it.

"I enjoyed the real estate talk, Chief. But I'm guessing we're done here."

"I guess we are. Just be careful, Dom. Help your friend out. Help us all out."

"Thanks for the heads up, Chief."

"It's for everybody's good."

Raul wondered just who the Chief included in his definition of everybody.

"That's good to know, Chief. It really is."

"No problem. You want a ride back out there?"

"No. Thanks. I need to work off breakfast."

"I should make that walk, too," Art said. "Too much sitting, my friend. Too much sitting."

15.

Jesse

Of course he didn't tell her everything.

He'd been honest about flunking out of ISU.

And selling weed.

Not about how much weed.

He didn't tell her about this other thing on the back burner.

He didn't mention it to Raul.

Or anybody he did nickel-and-dime business with.

He couldn't tell anybody.

It wasn't safe.

It was between him and a voice on the phone.

And he had to be careful because it was a deal that came from someplace else.

And it involved a process he didn't control.

It was even an accident that it was a deal at all.

Someone had run off and left a gap in a system that was dangerous with gaps.

But that created an opportunity.

And someone at the top of the pole reached way down to the bottom of the pole to do business with someone he'd never have done business with at all if there had been no gap.

Here we go.

16.

Art

For a minute he let the sun scrub his face and watched Dom walk toward the lake.

That's it — go talk to your friend.

Shape him up.

Warn him.

Persuade him.

Educate him.

Keep him out of my line of fire.

Why?

He didn't know.

Just a feeling.

Something for another day.

Not this day.

The boy had a good marching rhythm.

He knew that Nam vets called it humping.

You hump this. You hump that.

Troop was another Nam word.

Troop this and troop that.

He knew that from vets in Chicago who had their own dialect.

Had their own language, own culture.

Kept it far longer than helpful to adjust to civilization again.

"The world," they called it.

Art pulled out to head back to Argus.

He glanced at Dom a few times in the rearview mirror until he sank from sight.

Mr. Crankshaft sure had a mouth on him.

And a chunk of chip on his shoulder.

A whole Louisville Slugger of a chip.

Art knew that was just Vietnam talking.

Still whispering through the boy.

Still the breeze filling his sails.

He didn't think the boy was a bad sort at all.

He was prickly and defiant, but that was because he was still getting his feet wet.

The boy would certainly bear watching if he was drunk in a tavern.

No doubt about that.

He wouldn't take much shit from anyone about anything.

They all came back wounded in some way or another.

Attitude was all they had until they learned how to cry again.

17.

Raul

    He looked back one last time and saw the Chief's car disappear toward town.

    One foot in front of the other.

    Hump. To hump.

    To be humped.

    Keep a straight line. Economy of effort.

    Each step put him closer.

    To what?

    Home.

    Where was that?

    At the end of the road.

    Hump.

18.

Nicole

Nicole + Jesse =
Promise.
Hope.
Future.
Truth.
Anticipation.
Anxiety.
Fear.
Failure.
%
$
?

19.

Jesse

Jesse fired up the GTO and the dual exhausts barked loudly, the sound reverberating among the trees. It struck him as way too loud and he kept his foot light on the pedal. Instinctively he glanced around as though someone might be watching, then satisfied he was alone, he fired up a joint. May as well get a good charge going one last time for the ride into town to make that phone call. The phone call to make the deal. Jesse had made a promise that morning, one he felt sure he would break and hoped he would try again, maybe many times, to stop smoking dope. Or at least reduce intake for a while as part of an eventual withdrawal. That promised to be a real bitch and he was confident he would fail and wished rather than expected he would keep trying.

Nicole would like it if he quit or cut it down. She hadn't said anything, but he knew smoking weed was just a social thing with her. She could take it or leave it. Cutting it down to size might do him some good in her eyes. Women wanted you to do that shit — clean up, calm down, settle in, shape up, get civilized, cut your hair. The hair was off limits. He'd hang on to the freak flag. But the dope business had to go. He had sensed that for some time and Nicole's appearance just crystallized it nicely for him. She wouldn't do the dance with him long if she knew he dealt weed.

He wanted to quit.

Quit smoking it.

Quit selling it.

For the right reasons.

He didn't want to be a hermit in a trailer in the woods.

He had served his time.

But what was his crime?

He guided the GTO down the lane slowly, wondering where Raul had gotten to, but he decided he was around somewhere close. He felt it. His pack and stuff was still in the trailer. He might be down on the lakeshore, or taking a walk. He had all that Nam shit to work though. That seemed clear enough to Jesse, who otherwise couldn't imagine what it was like. Psycho-fucking-logical distress and all that. They came back angry, those Vietnam vets.

But angry at what?

Angry for having to go?

Angry because it was hot and humid and they had to truck around the jungle cutting though tangled shit with machetes and dodge snakes and God knew what else?

Angry that they got shot at, for sure.

Angry when someone got killed?

Of course.

But if you made it back with Sam the Salami, both balls, and all your arms and legs, shouldn't you feel pretty fucking good and not look back?

Jesse didn't understand the anger. He'd sold weed for a while the summer before to a Nam vet who lived in a farmhouse outside Bloomington. After the first buy Jesse always delivered to the guy because he didn't want him showing up at his trailer anymore. The guy had produced a

9 mm pistol one night and pointed it at Jesse. Just for the fuck of it, he said. Just horsing around, he said. It wasn't loaded and afterwards he even showed Jesse the empty clip and felt bad about it. He was awfully sorry. Jesse thought the guy might cry. He just carried the pistol, he said, because without it he felt like one leg was shorter than the other. But the one time was enough for Jesse. In the dope business he met too many dickheads and potential disasters.

Time to move on.

After this one deal.

A last, big deal.

Separation pay.

Seed money.

He horsed the GTO onto the road, pedal to the metal.

War.

When Jesse tried to picture war, all he saw was John Wayne in "The Fighting Seabees."

20.

Raul

He flagged Jesse down on the causeway.

"Good timing," Jesse said. He had a joint and passed it to Raul.

"Thanks, man." Raul took a deep hit. The guy sure starts early. "Hits the spot, actually."

"Why's that?" Jesse put the GTO in gear and squealed the tires a little.

Raul took a second deep hit and handed it back to Jesse. "Might want to slow down a bit, pardner."

"How come?" They were already coming up on the café to their left.

"The way you're going, you'll be on your cop buddy's tail in a few minutes."

Jesse eased off the pedal, glanced at Raul. They were coasting. "Say what?"

"I ran into the Chief in the café. He just left a few minutes ago. Maybe five minutes. Maybe less."

"He's in town by now." But Jesse still coasted.

"Probably," Raul said. "Unless he stopped on the way. Or maybe he's working his way back this way."

"Why would he do that?"

"He's a cop."

Jesse sped up to the first farmer's lane and turned around and they headed back across the causeway. "We'll take the back way to town."

"Do we need to go to town?"

"I do. I need to use the pay phone at Gilstrap's Texaco."

"Hot date?" Then Raul realized he knew better. "Or business?"

"I have to call a guy."

They went past the trailer and turned south at the T toward the dam.

"How much is in this car? Raul said.

"We smoked it."

"So what's the phone call about, then?"

Jesse fiddled with the radio station knob, then turned it off.

"It's the set-up call, right. Jesse? It's let's do a deal time, eh?"

"Something like that."

"Either it is or it isn't, man. You sound like some freaking secret agent."

"Did you talk to the Chief, Raul?"

"Did we talk? We practically wrote a play together, man. Lots of dialogue. Lots."

Jesse abruptly pulled off the county road down the lane to the dam and parked. They got out and walked over to the spillway. Water flowed swiftly over the dam's lip and down the spillway. Soggy leaves and tree limbs garnished with a few beer cans floated in the pool below.

"Tell me what he said. The Chief."

"He likes the potatoes at the café. Likes them pretty damn well. But he doesn't drink much coffee — too much caffeine." Raul figured to sweat Jesse a little. That's how the Chief worked it and it was good enough for getting information.

"He likes potatoes?" Jesse looked pretty confused to Raul.

"Well, they're pretty good potatoes, I have to admit."

Jesse nervously searched his pockets and found another joint.

"I thought we smoked it all," Raul said. The guy really chain-smoked that shit. He didn't think you could get addicted to dope. Must be a psychological addiction.

"I always carry a spare." Jesse lit it and sucked very deeply before passing it.

"Why not," Raul said.

"Tell me what the Chief said."

"He said you're quite the entrepreneur. That's pretty funny. The Chief has an interesting way of speaking."

"What did you say?"

"I played dumb. Said I didn't know whether you sold real estate or plumbing supplies. But he knows better, of course. Are you addicted to this shit, Jesse?" He passed the joint back.

"Addicted? I don't think weed's addictive. But I've been thinking about cutting back. Even quitting."

"Well, you're making a hell of an effort at it right now, man."

"That business about the Chief threw me off. What does he want?"

"No dope in his town. Pretty simple, really."

"That's it?"

"Pretty much."

"I don't sell in Argus. Never have."

"Very noble, Jesse."

"I wish it was. It's just too small to get away with."

"Especially with an eagle-eye Chief," Raul said. "I have to admit I don't quite get his look-the-other-way attitude, though."

"What do you mean?"

"The Chief said to tell you to keep your nose clean in his town. His town. But as long as you're basically invisible at the lake, he don't give a fuck. I think this Chief must be some sort of an idealist."

"What kind of idealist?"

"I'm not sure. Maybe the kind that has pretty much drawn up a list. This is OK, that's not. I go here, I don't go there. That kind of shit. Maybe idealist is the wrong word."

"Pragmatist?" Jesse said tentatively.

"Could be. Is that a writer's word, pragmatist?"

"Must be." Jesse grinned. "I remember it from college." They finished the joint.

"Tell me about the deal, Jesse."

"Not much to tell." He looked down at the floating debris in the spillway pool.

"Well, that's bullshit," Raul said. "Something like this, it has angles and complications. How'd you even get connected to it? Sort of a bigger pond than you're used to skating on, ain't it?"

Jesse shrugged, forced a fragile grin. "It's an accident, really. I get product from somebody who gets it from somebody else. One of the somebodies disappeared. Went to California, they said. They asked me to fill in. That's it."

In the Nam, Raul thought, that might get called an ambush at some point.

"Jesse, how much money we talking?"

"My cut's a couple thou just to be the middleman and get the product where it belongs. Plus a free taste of the cargo. A slice off it. That's worth another couple thou."

Raul whistled softly. "Decent bread for no work."

"Smart for him, too," Jesse said. "He didn't pay what I can get for that slice. But there're plenty of unknowns, risk. I don't really know the people I'll deal with."

Raul studied Jesse's face and saw the fear. He was glad to see that Jesse didn't think it was a lark on a sunny day for kicks. "Why are you doing it, Jesse?"

Jesse shifted from one foot to another and dug his hands deep into his jeans' pockets.

"I've got some bread put back. A few thou. I figure to sell off the whole inventory, plus this new deal, and walk into the sunset with a chunk of change. Start over."

"Start over," Raul said. "Start over and become a writer."

"I know it's not that simple, man," Jesse said.

"I'm glad to hear you say it," Raul said. "Because it's not."

"I know it," Jesse said.

"Do you even know what's out there beyond that sunset?"

"Nope. Not a clue, really. How much do I really need to know beyond it's time for something else?"

Raul remembered that he knew a thing or two about walking into unknowns.

"Fair enough. What can go sideways with this deal?"

"Everything," Jesse said. "Someone could get crazy. Someone could have a gun and get crazy. Someone could narc it out and the cops show."

"Sounds a little like the Nam," Raul said.

"Better weather," Jesse said with a grin.

"I'll grant you that, man. Is the deal just weed?"

"No. Hash, too. Some speed. Probably a lot of speed. Everybody's crazy for white cross these days."

Raul nodded. Crazy shit, he thought, but no crazier than the Nam. "When's this deal go down?"

"The weekend."

"Today's Friday," Raul said.

"Then probably tomorrow," Jesse said. "Or Sunday."

"Then you retire."

"Then I retire," Jesse said. "I guess so."

"And do what?"

"Been thinking of finishing college," Jesse said. "But probably not around here. After this deal, it would probably be best to move on. Too many people know me around here."

"Do you think you can just go and the past remain behind?"

"No. But you can't let that stop you from trying, right?"

"It's not some noble cause, Jesse."

"I know that. It's just a shitty little deal. But I'm already in up to my neck. A little more doesn't make much difference."

"No, I suppose it doesn't."

They got in the GTO and Jesse drove back to the main road.

"I could use some company," Jesse said after a few minutes. "On the deal."

Raul figured that was coming. He'd already made up his mind to go along, but he wasn't totally sure why. Maybe Jesse needed someone to look after him.

"Yeah. I'll go with you."

Jesse looked very relieved. "There's a few dollars in it for you, of course."

"That'll work itself out," Raul said. "Let's go make that call.

The Weekend

21.

Art

He saw the GTO pull in to Gilstrap's Texaco and Jesse James use the pay phone outside on a pole next to the air hose. Jesse was on the phone quite a while and Art could see him writing on a piece of paper. Mr. Crankshaft leaned against the car, arms crossed over his chest, eyes closed as the sun bathed his face. That one liked his sunbaths alright. He appeared not to even be there except in body. He thought momentarily of their talk at the café earlier and whether he'd really taken his advice and whether the two of them in town so soon meant a lot or not much at all. Then Art's mind drifted back to those spicy potatoes. They really were something. Was it sage they sprinkled on them? And dill? What was the spicy element, though? Just a dash of ground jalapeño, perhaps. He'd remember next time to find out.

Art was parked in an alley a block down from the Texaco. The car protruded just enough from the alley mouth that any moron with his eyes open ought to eventually catch sight of it. But Jesse James was too busy on the phone and Mr. Crankshaft maintained his zombie pose against the GTO. He knew where Mr. Crankshaft was in his head. Back in the swirl of it. He got that from a Nam vet he played basketball with in Chicago. The swirl. A swirl.

Combat, action, the shit — whatever it was called, it had a swirling quality to it. It was both very real and unreal at the same time. Surreal. It was loud then quiet, then loud again, and always chaotic. The man had struggled to articulate it to Art and finally concluded it was like being right smack in a tornado and somehow surviving and forever after hearing and seeing the swirl of it — and praying time would cut it down to something manageable.

He looked the other way down the street and saw Mayor Sullivan padding along toward the VFW on the next block. Must be getting on to lunchtime. He was still pretty full from breakfast and those awesome potatoes. Would they think he was crazy at the café if he swung by and got some to take home for dinner? He was the chief, after all, and people expected him to appear everywhere, and they didn't bat an eye over it. Most folks anyway, except those two yo-yos over at Gilstrap's hatching some deal. What else could it be? If he searched the car would he find too much evidence to ignore? Probably not. Jesse James was surely too smart for that. He likely was riding high and dry like an empty grain barge waiting to get filled up later.

Mr. Crankshaft finally dropped his arms and opened his eyes and just for the briefest second caught sight of the Chief and feigned indifference. It was subtle and quick and the Chief would have missed it altogether had he blinked just once. Then the boy dropped to a knee and adjusted a shoestring on his tennis shoes and took a better look. Too obvious, the Chief thought. You can do better than that. But the lad was already more than a month back from the swirl, that fine edge already eroding. They were a little careless, these two yo-yos. Whatever it was they were concocting, did they really think it could play out in his town?

Art watched Mr. Crankshaft — stop calling him that, he thought, because yo-yo worked just fine and fit the situation so much better — drift over to Jesse James and say something. Jesse looked up and stared square at the Chief and Dom (time to keep it real and call him by his name) gently placed a hand on his shoulder to turn his body away. The phone call was finished within a minute, but before they could get back in the GTO Art had pulled out onto Main Street and cruised by them slowly as they opened the doors and pretended not to make eye contact.

"Nice touch," Art said softly. "You just keep pretending you don't see me."

In his rear mirror from a block away he saw they still hadn't moved. They were gauging what he'd do, waiting to see if he turned around. Art instead turned at the next street and worked his way down a block and back up Adams to a spot he knew that was well-concealed by thick trees, but with a view of Main, and he parked. A couple minutes later the GTO slowly rolled by. Time to spook them some, he decided, and wheeled onto Main. He caught them easily because in their paranoia they were nailed dead on the speed limit and he rode their bumper several blocks, until the town had petered out and there was no traffic, and he pulled around, hit the lights, but kept on going past them, accelerating to 70 very quickly until they were no longer visible in the mirror.

He laughed out loud about the lights. That was a good touch. He'd contemplated the siren for a second, but decided not to hit it because he was still close to town and didn't want it to be an item of discussion. But the lights were good enough. They probably scared the holy shit out of them. Maybe Jesse James would have to clean the seats of that bad-ass GTO.

A few minutes later Art turned onto the lake road and went past the country café and chopped his speed momentarily to glance over, thinking again of those spicy potatoes. He'd have to stop for some on the return trip. There just wasn't time now, but he had decided he would get an order to go later. He had a strong hankering for some. He punched the accelerator and didn't slow down until he reached the causeway. The lake was calm and glassy and Art smiled in admiration as he puttered across the causeway and turned onto Jesse James' lane and parked with the cruiser pointed menacingly back toward the road.

22.

Jesse

"I thought we were dead meat for sure," Jesse said as they watched the Chief's car roar ahead of them and out of sight. "He freaked me out, man."

Raul nodded. "Well, he's gone now. Relax." Jesse's heart still raced and instinctively he reached into a pocket for a joint, but there weren't any more. "He was right on our bumper. Smack on it for three blocks."

"Two blocks," Raul said. "You were straight about no weed in the car, right? Not even a joint?"

"Scout's honor."

"Not even a reserve joint to your reserve joint?"

"I'm tapped out."

"Nothing under the tire in the trunk, or taped inside a wheel well?"

"In the wheel wells? No, but that's an interesting idea."

"Then what's the big deal?" Raul said. "He couldn't bust us for anything. Not even speeding. He was just fucking with us. Cops do that all the time, even to upstanding citizens, which we definitely are not."

"What are we?"

"Entrepreneurs," Raul said with a smirk. "The Chief's own definition."

"Not outlaws?"

"We're that, too, I'm afraid. Until this deal's over, anyway. Maybe longer. Maybe forever, man."

Jesse wondered what Raul meant by that, but he was still a little too agitated to pursue the thought very far or clearly. "Well, it will be over Sunday."

"Sunday? That's what the guy said?"

"Yeah. Sunday afternoon. He has to come from far away."

"Where?"

"He wouldn't say. Just that it was a drive."

"That's smart. Need to know and all that. Kind of military-like. Get in, drop the bomb, get out."

"Don't talk about bombs," Jesse said. "I'm nervous enough as it is."

"Just another deal, ain't it? Just bigger."

"I don't know any of these people," Jesse said. "And it means driving around with a powder keg of dope, so to speak. And speed. I'm used to knowing who will show up, and having just enough in my hand to do business. I'm small-time."

"Just figuring that out, Jesse?"

"Guess so." Jesse had never imagined being in over his head, but he knew it solidly now. He considered backing out. It was tempting to just call the guy back and bail out. Just move on. But the man had warned Jesse not to disappoint him and his tone had teeth to it. The deepest part of the river was always the middle and you had to submerge yourself a while to finally climb out on the other side. Then you could look back at the distant shore and wonder if your past had ever really happened at all and realize then was a frightening, sobering step in the process toward now.

Could the past be washed away?

Neutralized?

Or was it always there.

And old wound cloaked by scar tissue.

Well, he'd given his word.

Honor among thieves.

But without even honor among thieves, could there be honor with anyone else?

"What else do you know about this guy, Jesse?"

"Just that he'll be driving a blue Econoline van and we meet him at Bunnie's Tavern between noon and two."

"How will we know him?"

"He said he would know us."

"What is he, God?"

"No, Brant. His name's Brant."

"Brant?" Raul made a face. "That's his name? First or last?"

"Just Brant. That's what he said when I asked — just Brant."

"What the fuck kind of name is Brant?"

"Made up, probably," Jesse said. "We had a Brant when I was in junior high. He was always dicking around with black powder and blowing up little bombs in ditches."

Raul nodded. "I think I ran into him in the Nam, man."

"Really?"

"What do you think?"

"Right. Jesus — what if this Brant is the guy from junior high, though?"

"Then it'll be a reunion, man. We'll smoke doobies and sacrifice a goat or a pig to the gods."

"He wasn't much of a conversationalist," Jesse said. "I told him I have long blonde hair."

"But he knows your name, right, man? He knows you're Jesse Archer?"

"Yeah. Why?"

"Then if it was your bomber buddy from junior high he would have said something, don't you think?"

Jesse chuckled. "I guess that's right. Sorry."

Raul made a sour face. "Why Bunnie's Tavern? Whose idea was that?"

"He asked for some place public to meet that wasn't smack downtown. Said he would be driving straight through and would want someplace for a beer and food. So I said Bunnie's because it's on the edge of town. Was I wrong?"

"I guess not." But Raul seemed to chew on it a moment. "It's as good a place as any, I reckon."

"You're sure?"

"No, I'm not sure. But it has to start somewhere. You play the cards you get, aces or not."

Jesse pulled the GTO onto the shoulder.

"Raul, do we have any aces?"

"We? I'm just riding shotgun on this venture. You're the honcho. You're the money man."

"If you're in, then you have a say, Raul. Don't be a dick."

"I'm good at being a dick, man. Ask that Chief if I'm good at being a dick."

"We're past that," Jesse said. "I was asking if we had any aces."

"We can disappear to Florida. That's one ace."

Jesse wondered if he could do that — just top the GTO's tank and leave everything behind and flee, but decided he could not. And he wanted to see what Nicole was all about. Finally he had something to lose. Something worth getting and keeping and he figured to see things through.

"I've been to Florida," Jesse said. "Too sweaty. I don't know anyone there."

"Too much like the Nam for me," Raul said. "The Nam with shuffleboard and pink flamingos. So I guess we take that ace out of the deck."

"That just leaves getting it done and getting it over." Jesse pulled back onto the road. "Do they have flamingos in Vietnam?"

"I didn't see any."

"Maybe they were hiding," Jesse said.

"Could be. It did tend to get a little noisy over there. I was too wound up, I reckon, to check for flamingos."

"But you're OK now?" Jesse said.

"Did you think I wasn't?"

"I've been wondering about it, man. Sorry."

"That's OK. I'm adjusting. Don't know what else I can say about it."

"Good," Jesse said. "We don't have any flamingos at the lake, but there are plenty of ducks — and loons."

"Loons. That would be an unfortunate name to have. "

"We're not loons, Raul."

"What are we?"

"Entrepreneurs, remember?"

"We are that," Raul said. "Listen, why don't we go the back way to the lake. Maybe we avoid the Chief that way."

"Maybe we run into him coming back to town that way."

"Maybe. Life's a gamble."

"Where do you suppose he went in such a hurry?"

"Back to eat more of those damn spicy potatoes for all I know."

23.

Nicole

She picked up her paycheck at Ferguson's and was walking to the bank when she saw Jesse and Raul go by slowly in the GTO. She waved, then noticed that the police Chief was right behind them, very close to the GTO's bumper. Both cars rolled slowly down Main Street, the GTO a magnet pulling the Chief's cruiser along.

She crossed at the next intersection and looked up the street to see the Chief's light come on abruptly and his cruiser pull out from behind Jesse and haul ass out of sight toward the lake. Nicole stood on the corner in front of the bank for a few minutes to see if Jesse might come back. She knew the Chief must have been dogging Jesse for a reason, to make some point, but she wondered what it was. It was becoming sort of melodramatic. Very much so. Jesse the outlaw hounded by the sheriff. It was like a western on TV. Could a posse galloping frantically out of town be far behind? But westerns inevitably required a showdown on Main Street. What, then, had she just witnessed? She wasn't sure.

She wondered what he was thinking with the Chief dogging his bumper like that. What did she really know about Jesse?

It felt right.

She believed he had potential.

He could imagine being more than he was.

He was romantic, but not syrupy.

He was quiet, but not silent.

It felt right.

She trusted her feelings. That was essential, important. You could intellectualize things all day, but in the end, how do you feel? If you are honest and believe in loyalty and fidelity, and that life was an adventure best suited and most harmonious when you found a partner, a confidant — someone to love, as the song went — don't you want somebody to love, don't you need somebody to love, you better find somebody to love... then you trusted that feeling that bubbled up from someplace deep and you allowed it to play out.

She didn't know Jesse yet. Not really. But enough to feel he was one of the possibilities. Every one had a finite set of possibilities, Nicole believed — a small number of people you might meet during your life thanks to chance, the swirling winds of fate — crossing the street one day at a new intersection — or taking a strange road into a strange town, and any one of those people could be the one. And just as likely that one might not be available at that time.

Or, even though a person might be from that finite set, you never meet them because you turned left instead of right, chose one school over another, and so that person was a candidate only if you met them. A person in France could be one, but if you never go to France — finito. Or if you do go to France, maybe you don't go to a small town outside Paris because it's storming that day — finito.

Or, maybe you ask directions from a gendarme and turn down a quiet street, the wrong way, and a member of your potential set of suitors remains just a candidate on the street you should have chosen. And he might have been standing there, just 50 yards away, or at most 100 yards — meters in France, she remembered — and perhaps he was the owner of a grand restaurant, or even a — or he could be English, German, Danish, Swedish, American, Spanish, and just on vacation. You simply don't meet them, even though they technically are candidates, even though they virtually don't even exist because you haven't met them. Yikes! They are, but they also aren't. That was weird. They could be a member of the set, but at the same time practically don't exist because you never have tangible proof of their existence.

It was enough to conjure a headache. But that was what she believed. Jesse, she knew, was one from her finite set. Fate might have sent him down another girl's aisle every time instead of hers. She was confident her feeling on that was correct. But she knew it was not guaranteed. Jesse might prove only to be a test of her character, for example. He might be a member of the finite set, but a false signal of direction. A test. She would have to find out. That was the thing: you had to pursue these things to find out. If you didn't, you would never know. Jesse might be a total dead-end street. Or something much more.

It was an adventure.

And one factor, she knew, was what you brought to the mix.

It was like growing plants.

They needed to be nurtured, watered — talked to.

And then you sat back a little to see if they grew or wilted.

Jesse was a flower.

24.

Art

Art resisted the temptation to snoop around. He had no business in that rickety trailer. He was just a cop, not some medieval lord hovering over vassals. That was another man's home, as run-down as it looked. He had no evidence of a crime. That wasn't what this was about. What was it about? There was no design, no plan. It was about driving home the message. He couldn't count on Dom to be a reliable architect of that. Maybe it was also about covering his ass a little. That was always prudent, always smart, always necessary. He could even make notes about his talk with Dom, his trip today out to the trailer, to the outlaw's lair. He got a kick out of calling it that — outlaw's lair.

But notes would be a mistake. No paper trail. If it came to it, it would be enough to say he had taken steps. He had taken action. He had been on top of it, out in front of it. He'd monitored the situation. That's what all those trips to the lake were about, he would explain. The mayor would back him. He had that chip on the mayor to cash whenever he needed it. He was sure of it. As sure, anyway, as he could reasonably be. What he knew in his head was not what anyone else could know he knew. That sounded silly, actually. But it was enough that he knew what it meant.

The trees were coming back thick and green and limited his view of the lake. He figured he had some time so he got out and strolled to where the woods ended and the road to Kelton began and watched small whitecaps on the lake. There was just enough breeze for that, and it also ruffled branches and limbs above him in the trees. They made a very pleasant swishing sound, like people whispering secrets. From there he would see that cherry red GTO come across the causeway. Or maybe they would sneak home the back way. Maybe so. He couldn't discount that. Where would that come from? From Dom. Right. He might very well suggest that. He'd seen so much more of the world than that kid Jesse. Vietnam was still so fresh and vivid in Dom that he would be looking for a back way, safe haven, for quite a while. He probably hadn't been home long enough yet to get the smell of Vietnam out of his nostrils. So be it. Art calculated time and mileage, factored in some doper paranoia, and knew there was time to see them and to get back to his car. Sitting in the car would have an effect. So would standing beside it. He decided sitting was best. Let them ruminate a bit on whether he'd ever gotten out and snooped around.

And anyway, he knew there wouldn't be anything to see. If Jesse James was worth a damn at all as a doper, and he figured he was, there just wouldn't be anything in that trailer that could hurt him. Art looked back a moment at the thick woods. That's where it was, in there somewhere. Like a squirrel hiding nuts. Only Jesse James would know where the pot of gold was hidden. Pot of gold — that was a good one.

Art didn't care for the implications of going in a home without a warrant, without a real reason. That wasn't done. Not in his world. In Chicago it had sometimes been different. But that was more of a jungle than Argus. Far, far more. It had different rules, and ultimately Art had found the rules too onerous to live with. And the fallout from the rules. Remembering his Chicago days made him absently rub the little scar on his cheek where the bullet had teased him.

He glanced at his watch, then the causeway. He looked at the rolling whitecaps beckoning for a moment, then back at the clump of trees on the far side of the causeway where the road disappeared toward town. Nothing. So, it was the back way. Why not? That might have been his choice, too. He edged back into the woods, looking up a few times at the tall tops of the canopy, watched them sway and rub each other. He wondered how often deer eased up to the trailer at night, when there was no noise at all and the only light came from the trailer — from the outlaw's lair — and listened to the sounds of the only human for several miles — the music, no doubt, that sometimes poured from the trailer. Loud rock and roll. The Beatles, The Rolling Stones, The Who. Art liked those bands, but few people knew it. He had some of their albums. In the privacy of his home. Not for public consumption. He had been sorry, privately, to learn the Beatles were no more. It was all very recent. He'd heard about it on WLS out of Chicago one day in the police cruiser.

What did the deer and raccoons and possums think when The Beatles and The Stones and others filled their lonely woods? Whose woods these are I think I know. He was remembering Frost again, from school. The woods are lovely, dark and deep. But I have promises to keep, And miles to go before I sleep, And miles to go before I sleep.

He always liked that one a lot. It was a dense poem and the mood could be cut with a knife. Hell, a machete.

It was very dark inside that poem. He wasn't sure he understood poetry at all. That one offered all sorts of possibilities. Death, for example, though he had heard that was deceptive and not the case at all. He wondered about that a moment. What else was it about? He remembered, too, that teachers seemed to bleed the life out of poetry. All that jazz about metering. Iambic pentameter and all the rest. He remembered those things because they had quite a sound. So many syllables. But he never really understood it. He knew that rhythm was involved somehow. But wasn't all that iambic stuff really just mathematics? Math and poetry seemed an odd pair to him, like a tall man dancing with a very short woman. Rhyme he understood. But not all poetry rhymed. Much of it did not, though he couldn't say he had read a lot of it. Sometimes in a bookstore, not so very often, he would drift into the poetry section and read a few poems and ponder their meaning. He knew that in his police uniform, reading a book of poetry, he must have been quite the picture to some folks.

That particular Frost poem had stayed with him through the years. He was pleased that it had. It wasn't entirely true that you forgot what you learned in school. He'd also read some Hemingway in school, those tight little stories about the boy in Michigan trying to make sense of things. On the lake this day it could easily be a day for Hemingway, but that wasn't what he thought of. It was the Frost poem that lived inside him. He even recited it once during a black and lonely night off the coast of Korea as he gripped the ship's handrail and tried to see the coast, but it had proved to be invisible and the air was very crisp and the ship was blacked out and suddenly jets could be heard above, muffled swooshing noises, but not seen as they streaked inland and disappeared over the hills he knew were there but he could not see; and quickly the jets were very far away and barely audible and then he heard faint explosions, more like Fourth of July firecrackers than anything else. It was all taking place out in the dense blackness — out there. It was the blackest night he'd ever known, as black as in the Frost poem, though he was not depressed, just solitary, and as he heard the distant rumblings, that odd and haunting poem came to him, and he thought of the determined pilots in those jets, alone in their tiny bubble cockpits in a sea of blackness — and miles to go before I sleep.

He reached his car and got in and then tried to picture the lake he could not see very well at all through the foliage. He tried visualizing it without whitecaps and instead smooth, glassy, perhaps a sailboat or two — red and blue sails mixed with yellow and green — dotting the surface, slicing the water with small bow waves. It was such a pleasant picture. He thought again of the house he might buy on the lake in a few years. He would not need much of a boat. Certainly not some big cabin cruiser or ski boat. Or one of those squat little family barges that lumbered along with beer-bellied drunks clutching Budweisers in their little Styrofoam holders, hooting and hollering, and falling overboard sometimes. That always struck him as ignorant, in a way. Something small and sleek, with a modest motor, for puttering around on sunny days in the calm bays out of the wind, would be just fine. And with a fine, elegant wife, too, that he believed — and ardently hoped — he would eventually find. But he would want a solid pier of his own at this lake house so he could lead his wife by the hand and they could stroll barefoot along its warm wooden planks baking in the orange sun and lean against a guardrail, like that night on the ship in the dark, but not alone and with the light of the world illuminating the lake.

25.

Raul

They didn't see the Chief's cruiser until well up the lane. He had turned it around between some trees and it was pointed directly at them like a missile ready to erupt into flight, Raul thought. He could see a subtle smile on the Chief's face through the clean windshield. He glanced at Jesse, who turned off the GTO and sat back in his seat, sighed heavily, and brushed strands of blonde hair away from his face. Raul was surprised that Jesse seemed fairly calm.

"Well," Raul said. "You were wondering where the Chief had gotten to."

"He's not a hard man to find at all," Jesse said. "Just look out your door and there he is."

The Chief opened his door and slowly got out, but he didn't start toward them. He appeared content to rest a hand on the hood of his cruiser and look at them expectantly. His smile had spread some.

"At least he's smiling," Raul said, evaluating the possibilities.

"He's a friendly guy," Jesse said. "I guess he's not at the café eating those famous potatoes."

"No, he definitely ain't eating those damn potatoes. C'mon, let's get out. Don't let him have the upper hand by just sitting here."

"He doesn't already have the upper hand?"

"Remains to be seen. C'mon. He's not in a hurry."

They got out and walked over to the Chief.

"Long time no see," the Chief said. He leaned against his car and crossed his arms across his chest.

"But it seems like just a few minutes, really," Raul said. Might as well stick it back at him, he figured. The Chief seemed to sort of enjoy banter. Out of the corner of his eye he caught Jesse looking beyond the Chief, into the woods, and knew Jesse was wondering about his stash, wondering if the Chief had even found it. Raul hoped Jesse was good at hiding things. He guessed the Chief didn't even bother to look for it. He was unconcerned about it, it seemed.

The Chief glanced at his watch. "A half-hour, actually. But who's counting?"

"Not us," Raul said.

"What can I do you for, Chief?" Jesse said.

Raul smirked. Good one, kid. That's the spirit. He thought the Chief appeared to enjoy it, too, as he nodded at Jesse.

"You should be a car salesman, Jesse," the Chief said.

"I don't think I'm cut out for sales, Chief."

"Not what I hear." The Chief had dropped the smile.

"Depends on what you hear," Jesse said.

Raul was impressed. Jesse had found some backbone. This Chief didn't strike him as a man to trifle with when things counted.

"I don't hear much," the Chief said, momentarily looking down at the ground then sharply back at Jesse. "But I can see a lot. I've got good eyes."

Jesse returned the stare. "This a social call, Chief?"

"Let's call it that, if you like," the Chief said. "But we need to have a serious conversation. You've got time for that, do you?"

"All the time in the world," Jesse said.

"Good. I appreciate the hospitality, Jesse."

"How can I refuse the chief of police?" Jesse said.

"You can't," the Chief said. "Bad form if you did."

Raul finally realized the Chief really was just there to talk and he relaxed a little. If he'd found the stash things would have started off far differently.

The Chief turned to Raul. "Why not drag those lawn chairs over, Dom, and we'll get comfortable."

"Just like buddies."

"Just like," the Chief said.

Raul felt a little put out at being directed by the Chief. This wasn't the damn Army anymore. But he also found the Chief frankly hard to dislike. He was trying but seemed to always fall a little short. He would have to try harder, see where it led. But not too hard.

"Glad to oblige, Chief. Getting comfy is just the thing for a good talk. Like fraternity brothers."

"You're a corker, Dom," the Chief said as though Raul wasn't there at all.

"Part of my charm, Chief."

"So, you actually have some?"

Raul knew that one was best left alone.

Jesse made his boldest move yet. "How about a beer, Chief? There's PBR in the fridge."

The Chief eased into his chair slowly and the smile came back. "Bring me one."

Interesting, Raul thought. He was breaking bread. Accepting the pipe in the wigwam. Letting down his hair.

This Chief was full of surprises. He was a hard man to categorize.

"Chief, ain't you on the meter, so to speak?" Raul said. "Drinking on the job?"

The Chief's eyes narrowed slightly and very briefly, like some red-tail hawk eyeing potential prey from a tree limb.

"I'm not on the job right now, Dom. Not officially. I clocked out." He accepted the can of Pabst from Jesse and took a small sip, but couldn't decide at first which hand to keep it in.

Raul wondered if that off the clock stuff was true or just bullshit. It didn't really matter. It was just a verbal volleyball.

"Do you actually do that, Chief? Clock in and out in one of those cute little time clocks? In at eight, out by five, and all that?"

"Not exactly," the Chief said and his tone signaled the end of that discussion thread.

"Just curious," Raul said, but the Chief was studying the ash remains of the campfire.

"Must be damn pleasant to sit by the fire out here, boys. Cozy and warm. I've got a good fireplace in town, but it's not quite the same. Not really."

"Hard to beat a good fireplace, though — eh, Chief?" Raul could picture the man warming his feet in front of the fire, maybe sipping a Scotch. Raul figured him for a Scotch man.

"True," the Chief said. "But you don't get the smells, the aromas, like you do around a good roaring campfire. And the stars. Out here you can probably see them very well."

"Stars up the ying-yang out here, Chief," Raul said. "Out the wazoo."

The Chief looked up. "But these trees are a problem. You'd need to find a clearing for a good view."

"So true," Raul said.

"I could build a fire," Jesse said abruptly. "There's wood leftover from the other night."

The Chief studied Jesse a moment. "Go ahead if you like, Jesse. But I really don't think I'll be here that long."

That's it — get in, get out, and let everybody know how it's going to be, Raul thought. Deal from strength and watch your back. Sort of like the Nam. Raul wanted the Nam to go away and hoped, finally, it was beginning to fade some, like aging jeans that took an awful lot of washing to finally appear bleached clean.

"So, what can I help you with, Chief?" Jesse said.

"I can help you," the Chief said. "Find another business, son." The Chief leaned forward in his chair. "Get out of the one you're in."

Direct and emphatic. Raul noted it wasn't a suggestion, but also not a venomous threat. The Chief's a plow straight-ahead guy. Raul looked at Jesse to gauge his reply. Be careful, he thought.

Jesse didn't say anything at all. He just stared back at the Chief, who took another sip and leaned back.

"Jesse's been thinking of going back to college, Chief," Raul said, a little surprised at himself.

The Chief looked pleased and nodded. He shifted his PBR can to the other hand.

"That's a fine idea, Jesse."

"And he's got a girlfriend now," Raul said.

"That gal from Ferguson's," the Chief said. "I know."

"We just met," Jesse said. "I don't really know her that well."

"Don't let that stop you son," the Chief said. "It all starts off modestly. Good things start small."

"They do," Raul said. Was he suddenly a town elder?

"What would you study in college, Jesse?" the Chief said. "Where would you go?"

Raul thought Jesse looked a little like a tourist in a foreign country attempting to understand directions in a language he did not know. It was amusing, but also sad. What emotion was the Chief feeling? Was he amused? Did he enjoy power over Jesse? The Chief's face was stony, not betraying much thought at all. That was the official Chief, though. There was more to him, like an iceberg with so much submerged. Raul didn't dislike him at all, but he reminded himself that submerged icebergs ripped open hulls.

"I don't know," Jesse said. "I went a year at ISU already."

"Then just three more years to go," the Chief said. "Those years could go just like that." He snapped his fingers for emphasis. "What did you study, son?"

"I just took classes. Whatever sounded good."

"How'd you do, Jesse?"

Jesse looked at Raul, then sighed slowly. "I flunked out. What can I say?"

"No shame in it, son," the Chief said. "None at all."

That wasn't true, Raul thought. There's plenty of shame in failure. It cuts deep. It's what you did about it that made all the difference.

"Did you go to college, Chief?" Jesse said.

"I didn't. I joined the Navy right after high school in Chicago. I'd seen enough of the city and I wanted to see some of the world."

"You saw it," Raul said. "You saw Korea."

"I saw the coast of Korea, and Seoul once. I suspect there was a whole lot more between them."

"I hear you," Raul said, remembering the green coast of Vietnam, and Saigon. "Call me Raul, Chief. If you like.

That's my nickname. I never cared that much for Dominick, or even Dom."

"Raul? It's Spanish, right? How'd you get it?"

"Gave it to myself. Dominick and Dom sound like a Catholic priest. Father Dom, Father Dominick. And having people say Dominick Artemis Cruikshank more than once or twice is punishment."

"That's a mouthful alright," the Chief said. "Raul it is. It's got a good long breath to it for a short name." He finished his beer and got up. He looked for a place to put the can.

"Here, Chief," Jesse said, standing up. "I'll take it."

"Thanks, Jesse." He looked at Jesse a few seconds and then slipped his hands into his jacket pockets. "Any questions, son?"

"No, I reckon not." They made eye contact for a few more seconds.

The Chief turned to Raul. "What do you figure to do with yourself, Raul, now that you're settled back into town?"

"I haven't given it much thought." Raul felt doltish for such a blatant lie.

"I doubt that," the Chief said. "I really do. But if you ever want to talk about it, come see me." He walked to his car and opened the door. "You know where to find me."

"Eating those spicy potatoes," Raul said.

"You're a hoot, Raul. A real hoot."

"Thought I was a corker."

"Both."

"For sure."

The Chief smiled, threw Raul a casual salute, then got in and drove slowly down the lane and pulled onto the road to town. He flashed the overhead lights once and Raul chuckled.

"The Chief always gets the last word," Raul said.

They sat back in their chairs and Raul later realized it must have been nearly five minutes before either of them said anything at all.

26.

Art

He pulled into the café's lot, still snickering over hitting his lights when he left the trailer. That was a nice touch, he thought. He even laughed out loud once and the waitress smiled and asked what the joke was. He knew he probably got a rise out of that Raul. That boy was indeed a hoot and a corker, and a bit of a prick, too, but Art understood where it came from and mostly let it wash off his back. Art had been a lot like him at that age, in that blurry interval just after Korea and before he became a cop in Chicago. Raul just needed a sense of purpose. He needed to belong to something. If he had it, the attitude ought to fade. The boy had washed the soil of Vietnam off long ago; now he just needed to sort of let the rest of it drain out of his mind and dry up and dissipate into the breeze. Art believed he could help him in that department, but it was all up to the boy. Like some wary alley cat, it had to be his idea, or at least the illusion of it.

Art decided to eat his potatoes at the café instead of taking them home. He wasn't in a hurry. He was feeling relaxed, calm. He felt he had accomplished something with Jesse. He hoped, anyway. You never knew. You did your best and then believed it would work. He looked around: it was very cozy and not too well-lit inside the cafe, and there was only a smattering of customers, the hum of conversation not too loud, not frantic. A few folks waved or stopped by his table for a very quick hello. They seemed to know not to hover when the Chief was eating. That came with the job. That could be called a fringe benefit, but he wouldn't abuse it. He had never signaled impatience. Art would not be rude to the people he served. He was grateful for the life they provided him.

After the waitress cleared his plate he drank coffee and swiveled his chair so he could gaze out the window. It was the weekend and he pondered a strategy for spending it. He had agreed to drop by the Catholic church for the Friday night service. That was part of the job, too, but it wasn't all business. Church was where a single man of station could expect to meet single ladies, something he had quietly been pursuing under the cover of visiting all the Argus churches. He was not Catholic and didn't think the rather strict Catholic doctrines were for him, but the few times he'd visited Catholic churches in Chicago he enjoyed the pageantry of it all. Those churches had been immense, cavernous, with much wondrous stained glass and a strong, peasant smell from the wooden pews. What kind of wood were they made of? Nothing cheap, he figured. He would ask Father Malinowski at the service. The father seemed like a good man and liked a shot of whiskey at the VFW. Art liked it that Catholics would take a drink, unlike some of the Baptists he knew. He was not picking on Baptists. But many of them were just too tightly wound.

Maybe church was what Raul needed. That was up to him. Art did not like religion foisted on him and would not do it to others. That was at the very root of the world's problems, he thought. He winced at the notion of people in Ireland, or the Middle East, slaughtering each other over religion. What was the Irish divide — Protestants and Catholics? He wished he knew more about their differences. Probably there was more to it than just religion — politics, to be sure; but religion was a big part of it and there was never a shortage of Crusaders or religious warriors of any stripe ready to leap into flaming cauldrons to advance their cause.

But God must surely adopt many forms, to many different people. An accommodation by a benevolent and wise power that could not be imagined or neatly bottled for submissive consumption, despite the sweaty efforts of Baptist and Pentecostal ministers he encountered in particular. He could even imagine a day when a future president might hitch his wagon too close to faith and try to drag the whole country behind it. That would not be good at all. Nixon seemed to be immune from that so far.

What did Jesse need? Religion? A harder question. He felt some sort of brotherhood with Raul, for example, though he was technically old enough to be either one's father. He was nearly forty and they were about 22 or so. Raul would be slightly older. Yes, it was technically possible. He did not feel particularly fatherly toward Raul, though. It was indeed more of a brotherhood of shared experience — war and its attendant mental adjustments. Art had seen a gun pointed at him in anger, with intended malice, and perhaps Raul had been shot at, too. He did not know and did not really need to know. He conceded that Raul probably saw more war than he had. Art smiled at the notion: he'd seen almost nothing of the war in Korea. He heard it a few times, far off and abstract. He'd seen a cluster of blackened, crushed buildings on that one trip to Seoul, but they were far outside the city, to the north, a brief side trip with other sailors so they could later say they saw "the front." Then they were back on their ships, only the occasional sound of jets overhead, those angry hornets that never stayed in sight very long at all.

Raul had spent his tour "in country," he knew from the grizzled, beery vets of older wars at the VFW. There was no "front" to Vietnam, just body counts and search and destroy, and he knew Raul had seen at least a sliver of all that toward the end before coming home less a broken egg than many others.

Jesse was something else altogether. He had not really been forced to grow up in a hurry, like Raul. He was no kid anymore, but not yet fully a man. What did you call folks in between? Manboys? Boymen? He'd seen a few of them in the Navy. But the Navy forced them to grow overnight. Jesse had drifted. Apparently he lived in a marijuana cloud with a rock and roll soundtrack and still hadn't seen through the illusion of making a few bucks at something unsubstantial and illegal. And it wasn't so much that it was illegal, Art reminded himself. It wasn't so much of that at all, which often worried him some, despite his rather casual feelings on the subject. It was the thinness of it, the remarkable inertia of it. Sitting around in a haze in a trailer and selling a dried plant to pimply-faced townies and know-it-all college students for enough money to buy beer and frozen pizza and rock albums.

Why did he want to help Jesse?

If he could articulate that clearly, and he couldn't yet, he felt he would also know himself very well, and so it was well worth the effort. He settled his bill, left a generous tip, and walked outside. He stood in the doorway a moment and enjoyed the sunshine with his eyes closed, like he had seen Raul doing that day at Ferguson's. When he opened his eyes he saw Jesse's red GTO go by toward town.

26.

Jesse

"That was the Chief's car," Jesse said as they went past the café.

"What was your first clue?" Raul said.

Jesse looked in his mirror to see if the Chief's car moved.

"My first clue was the sign on the door that said Argus Police. And the Chief standing in the doorway, watching us go by."

"Did he wave?"

"No."

"You should be a detective," Raul said. "Maybe the Chief will hire you."

Jesse laughed. "With a degree in criminal justice, I could do that."

"And a haircut," Raul said.

"That, too."

"Maybe that's your calling, Jesse. You already know the criminal mind."

Jesse didn't appreciate the remark. "Now you're in the pool, too. Welcome to the deep water."

"I guess I am. Sorry."

Jesse chafed some at Raul's comments. The guy could be pretty caustic sometimes and Jesse tried to cut him some slack because he knew guys back from Vietnam were a little crazy and needed time to cool off and all that. But still, if they were really becoming friends, Raul needed to cut him some slack, too. Jesse didn't think of himself as a criminal any more than the speakeasy owners of Prohibition were criminals. Sure, it was technically true that speakeasies broke the law, but it was a law many disagreed with, and it didn't last. He'd read all about it in college. There could be a day when marijuana was legal, Jesse believed, and besides, it was simply hypocritical to allow alcohol but not weed. Make them both legal, or outlaw them both. He had said that many times to people even though he always understood that legal weed would put him out of business. What the fuck, he thought, it's a going-out-of-business sale on the horizon anyway.

They made the turn toward Argus to buy more steaks for another feast over the open fire — Raul's idea this time. Jesse checked his mirror repeatedly, but no Chief's car appeared.

"I expected to see him by now," Jesse said.

"The Chief? Naw. He's done with us for now. Said his peace and all that."

"What makes you so sure?"

"That's how it is with guys like him. They do what they think is right and expect good results. Then they go home and watch Johnny Carson on TV and sleep like babies."

Jesse mulled it. "The Chief's an idealist?"

Raul looked out his window. "Sort of. Principles matter to him." He looked back at Jesse. "What do you think of him?"

Jesse recalled that fear was his first reaction to the Chief, but he didn't stay scared long once the Chief sat down with him.

"I kind of like him, Raul. He seems like a good man. Can't deny he's cut us some breaks."

"He's cut you most of the breaks, but I hear what you're saying."

"Do you like him, Raul?"

"The Chief?"

"No, Ho Chi Minh."

"Funny." Raul looked back out the window at the sprouting corn. "Yeah. I do."

"Ho Chi Minh, or the Chief?"

"Forget about being a detective, Jesse. Comedy is your golden path."

"Well, I'm going to need something after all this."

"College, man," Raul said. "College ought to fix you right up. Even the Chief says so."

"It didn't the first time."

"That was a couple years ago. You're different now. Aren't you?"

"Maybe so," Jesse said. Something did feel different. "What about you? Thought about school?"

"If we survive the weekend, I'll give it my undivided attention."

"The Chief's visit sort of complicates things, don't it?"

"I'd say," Raul said. "You should tell Nicole. You know that, right?"

Jesse had been thinking of Nicole, but hoped to avoid bringing her into the deal in any way.

"Might be best to leave her in the dark, Raul."

Raul fished in the glove box, looking at eight-tracks. "Let me tell you the one thing I know about women, Jesse."

"You only know one thing?"

"Only one I have confidence in. You don't want to start off on the wrong foot, and lying, or call it keeping a secret — whatever, that's the wrong foot forward."

"Too late for that."

Raul glanced at Jesse. "What do you mean?"

"Well, I fessed up that I sold weed, but I didn't say how much."

"Now you can. It's not too late. But you need to get her on board before the deal, not after. That way she doesn't feel bamboozled, or whatever."

"What's it to her?" Jesse said. "I mean, really. What's it matter if she knows or not?"

"You can say you didn't want to tell her at first because you didn't want to worry her. Sort of gives you an out. But you changed your mind because you realized you want to be honest — had to be honest. That's romantic, I think. Women eat that up."

"You're an expert?"

"You know weed, I know women. Well, a little."

"Just enough to be dangerous?"

"Just enough to be careful."

In town they cruised slowly by Ferguson's and Jesse saw Nicole through the window, at her register. He honked the horn and she whirled around and waved back. Then she motioned for them to park and come in. After they parked and walked to the front door of Ferguson's, Jesse glanced down the street and saw the Chief's car come into town, then turn down a residential street.

"The Chief."

"I saw him," Raul said. "That's his street, I think. He lives down there. He's just going home."

"You think?"

"How would I know?" Raul said. "We can stand out here and wait, if you like. Or go find him. Maybe invite ourselves in for tea, listen to some of his Lawrence Welk records."

"No thanks," Jesse said. "The Chief always seems to know where we are."

"Relax, Jesse. Things are pretty quiet for now."

"All quiet before the storm," Jesse said as they went in.

28.

Nicole

Something was up. It was in the air molecules swirling around them — following them like a tiny cloud. A gray cloud signaling rain. Jesse and Raul played at being cool, calm, and collected, but Nicole sensed something unsaid. It was in their tone, their body language. They'd made quite the haul of groceries for the night's cookout, made jokes and bantered about the right steak sauce and such, but she just felt they were covering up something and she was determined to discover what it was. The Chief was in on it, too. Had to be. The three of them seemed to attract each other like magnets.

The Chief came in to shop a couple hours after Jesse and Raul left. He rolled into her aisle quietly, distracted, as though he'd forgotten something and just couldn't remember what it was. His cart was full and Nicole though it looked like it had been filled impulsively, even randomly. She was just a little taken aback when he asked how Jesse was. The Chief had a habit of appearing serious when maybe he wasn't, and vice versa, she thought. He was quiet in the store — always friendly enough, though — but his quiet always seemed to speak volumes. She knew people admired him, felt secure because of him. But he was hard to know and she felt she had less insight on him than anyone who passed through her aisle.

After work she went home and showered and changed into faded bell-bottoms and a red halter, but with a nice blue blouse over it. She fussed with her hair and was finally satisfied with it and then made her special German potato salad for the cookout. The recipe was handed down from her German grandmother, who'd come over from Frankfurt and who spoke almost no English. On the way out she resolved not to sleep with Jesse that night. She wanted to. She knew that almost immediately. But there were standards to meet. There had to be standards and limits. She would diplomatically but firmly put her foot down on the fact that cookouts were not dates. They were fun and she had already learned much about Jesse, and Dom, too, smoking a little weed and listening to tunes; but they were most definitely not real dates.

A date was when the boy — man — came to the door of your house and rang the bell and did his best to impress your parents with his civility, his manners, and even potential. That was a date. Well, the beginning of one. After that, it became a date only if you went to a movie or dinner, or both. Or over to ISU to see a concert. Or a play. Playing miniature golf could be a date if you had a burger before or after — or a pizza. Going to a tavern, say Bunnie's, could be a date. Sort of a semi-date. A full date if he bought food and invited you to play pinball or pool or darts.

Hanging out in smoky cars at Gilstrap's Texaco downtown was definitely not a date. Cruising county roads smoking weed, blaring Led Zeppelin, and avoiding the county sheriff was definitely not a date. The cookout was absolutely a step up from hanging at Gilstrap's or cruising county roads because it involved preparing a meal, making some effort at socialization, conversation. Still, a cookout was what it was: a pleasant encounter, but not a real date.

When she pulled up Jesse's lane it was twilight and a fire was already roaring and she saw that someone had strung Christmas lights from one tree to another. Green, red, and yellow lights sparkled like stars fallen to earth. Nicole thought they were very pretty. It was a nice touch. A very grand touch.

But a cookout still wasn't a real date.

29.

Art

Art had thought briefly of taking the long and scenic way home, around the lake, but decided he just wanted to be done with the cop business for the day and go home. He drove leisurely to town, stopping briefly to chat with a farmer tinkering with a tractor by the side of the road. The man had smiled and wiped his forehead with a handkerchief and told Art he didn't need any help and so Art went on in to town and turned down his street and sat a moment in his driveway. He expelled a long sigh that had been all morning in formation. He'd said his piece with Jesse and Raul. That was that. The ball was in their court. He sensed they were up to something. The old cop sense. Cop's suspicion. He was usually right about those things. Whatever it was Jesse and Raul were doing, he hoped it was minor. Maybe it was nothing. That could very well be. He'd been wrong a few times in that department. But not many.

In the shower he let the warm water wash the day off him. Steam filled the bathroom as though it was a sauna. He lingered, his head under the shower head for a good dunking. The water rejuvenated him and afterward he put on crisply creased khaki slacks and a blue, button-down Oxford shirt and a leather belt and slipped into Thom

McCann loafers. No tie. Art wasn't a tie sort of man. He always felt like he was slowly strangling in a tie. Funerals and weddings required it, but otherwise he didn't bother. In civvies, a tie would still make him feel like a cop.

He ate a nice early dinner of leftover pork chops, peas, and carrots, and he even made a small salad with Roquefort dressing. He drifted through his house, looking for something but not quite knowing what. Out on the porch, he looked at his watch, saw he had time before church, impulsively got in the car, and drove to Ferguson's to stock up on groceries. Mostly, he decided, he just needed to move for a while and not sit. There would be enough of that in the church pew, later. There would be too much of it.

He roamed aisles at Ferguson's and chatted briefly with citizens. Some of them remarked that he looked very different in civilian clothes and several times he snuck looks at himself in the mirrors behind the produce coolers. He would adjust his belt and tuck his shirt into his pants tighter. Art was impulsive in his choices, filling the cart far more with what looked interesting than what he needed. When he looked up in the checkout aisle, he saw it was Nicole behind the register.

"Good afternoon, Chief," she said, looking just a tad wary, he thought.

"Well how are you?" Art said. "Just call me Art if you like. The Chief's off the meter."

His items crowded the conveyor belt: maraschino cherries, green and black olives, fresh catfish fillets, steaks and chops and lean hamburger, a variety of sauces and relishes and other condiments, two bottles of Mateus wine, frozen TV dinners, canned chili, canned beans and ham soup, a gaggle of seasonings, heads of lettuce, tomatoes, cucumbers, onions, green and red peppers, razor blades, shaving lotion, shampoo, three kinds of bar soap, four varieties of salad dressing — Thousand Island, French, Roquefort, and Ranch — a new sauce pan and spatula, a cheap set of four wine glasses — even a new broom and mop.

Nicole called for a stock boy to help bag and then put all the bags in a cart. As Art wheeled the cart away, he turned back to Nicole and said matter-of-factly, "Tell Jesse hello for me. Have a nice day."

At home he put everything away in cabinets and the fridge and washed the new wine glasses before putting them on a shelf and concluded he was well provisioned. He recalled momentarily the queer look Nicole had when he mentioned Jesse. It would get back to Jesse, and it was supposed to. Before going to church, he thought to grab a navy blazer. He would carry it, to imply a sense of propriety — to convey he certainly understood those things — but he had no plans to wear it. It was warming up and the church would be even warmer with all those people. He would tuck it rather casually under an arm as he pocketed a hand and people would notice it, know he could wear it, see that it was a blazer and a touch of formality but also realize he was the Chief and could get away with not wearing it.

He pulled up a little early at the church, as Father Malinowski himself was arriving, and the two of them climbed the steep stairs to the church together.

"How goes it, Father?"

"It goes well, I think. I can feel the summer finally coming. I enjoy the warmer weather."

"Spring stayed a while," Art said.

"Change can be slow, Chief. Sometimes it needs longer to unfold."

Art was always uneasy when ministers and priests and pastors talked cryptically. They all shared that habit. You never knew if a rose was just a rose, or something else. And he disliked the practice of replying in kind with something cryptic, but expected.

"I guess without that longer time, though, Father, change might be flawed or even false."

Art thought that Father Malinowski seemed to chew on that a moment.

"Only time can tell," the priest finally said as he opened the church's massive door and beckoned for Art to enter. Father Malinowski disappeared to do whatever it was he did to prepare to stem the tide of evil and immorality.

Inside, Art was much happier. He always enjoyed inspecting the artwork and architecture of a church. It was as though, he decided, that he was as riveted by the structure of a good church as he was ambivalent about its messages. A gun, he thought, could be beautiful, well-made, but still deliver an awful message. He had to admit that was a rather odd image. He inspected the colors but not so much the design of the stained glass and smelled the wonderfully rich aroma from the polished wood of the pews and walls. He resisted sitting in a pew until almost the very moment Father Malinowski appeared and noisily cleared his throat to begin the Mass. Art had chatted with townspeople amiably, taking notice of several attractive women he knew to be single before finally choosing a place in a pew near one of them, but not too close to Father Malinowski's voluminous lectern.

Art thought Father Malinowski had a pleasant and rich voice, but later, if asked, he would have been compelled to say that he did not quite recall what the homily was about. He heard the words, but they did not really sink in. He dozed with his eyes open throughout, looking around a couple times to gauge the reactions of others. Everyone seemed riveted by the homily, or perhaps they were just better at sleeping with their eyes open; but he suspected that most of them were really listening to the sales pitch and buying the product. Many nodded vigorously, or glanced at each other with frowns.

Midway through the homily, Art managed to keep his chin up while clearly daydreaming, again entertaining his longing to live out on the lake. He was a decent swimmer and hoped that he might buy a place, when the time was right, of course, that offered good swimming. Sand could be brought in if necessary, the shore graded, rocks removed. A few quality lawn chairs — not the cheap kind from K-mart — would look nice around one of those large umbrella things. There he would relax with a drink — maybe a tequila sunrise or rum and coke — after a brisk swim, the water still beading on his forehead and trickling down his neck. If he was fortunate enough to find a wife by then, she would come down the brick walkway to the beach, on bricks he laid himself, to join him with more drinks and the towel he would forget to take.

He could almost visualize the house and how it should be. It must have a very large picture window, or even several, so he could sit in an easy chair with a book and look up as he pleased to watch the sun reflect off the water. The house might be a Cape Cod. His home in town was Tudor and he could not recall seeing anything like that on the lake. Maybe he could have a Tudor built. It didn't have to be Tudor. He liked Tudor, but that was not set in stone. Not at all. He made a note to ask one of the contractors in town, very casually — perhaps as just idle chatter at the VFW — what it cost to build a nice house. They would have many designs. Probably there was a style he did not even know of that would strike him immediately as the one.

He felt sure the house was just a matter of when and then getting started; he was far less sure about a wife, though hopeful. He glanced at the woman he'd chatted with before the homily, the one with long auburn hair. She was five years younger than him and had lost her husband five years ago. The math suited him. He felt someone younger was best. The age difference was compatible and he felt that the five years likely meant she had also grieved sufficiently and moved on. She taught English at Argus High and so she was smart, articulate. They had chatted pleasantly and she had smiled often and toyed absently once with a curl of hair at her pink ear. Art smiled broadly and recalled that in high school all the boys were sure that when a girl played with her hair and smiled, she liked you. She had even cocked her head to one side a little as he spoke, as though she was angling herself to hear him better. It could be a sign that said: I am listening to you and you have all of my attention because I really want to hear what you have to say.

Art reflected on why he had never married. There certainly had been plenty of women. He knew women found him to be handsome and athletic, though he still fretted slightly over the lack of exercise and a couple extra pounds and he resolved to try running or swimming at the high school pool. When he lived in Chicago, he met lots of women in taverns and police association dances. He'd gotten involved with another officer's wife once and felt very poorly about it, but always reminded himself that they were separated at the time and he could not know for sure they would get back together; but they did and it left a bad taste. He also felt that Chicago women had too much of the city in them. They were in too much of a hurry to be somewhere, anywhere. He believed that Argus women were more realistic. They knew life wasn't perfect, could not be perfect. That was important to him. People had to be realistic about what life offered. There was just so much that could be done, could be realized.

After the service, Art shook hands with Father Malinowski and complimented him on the stirring homily. He walked the woman with auburn hair — Carolyn — to her car and made a date for coffee after church Sunday. When he got home he changed into pajamas and poured a glass of wine in one of his cheap new wine glasses and fell asleep in his easy chair until it was time to go to bed.

30.

Raul

After they ate, Raul excused himself for a walk under the stars to give Jesse and Nicole some privacy by the fire. He could see they were in that questions and answers phase of best behavior and curiosity and wonder. Raul was happy for Jesse, though he sensed that Nicole was the brains of the outfit. He grabbed a cold PBR and went down to the lakeshore and sat on a causeway rock and smoked the joint Jesse had slipped him as he left.

To the south in the darkness he could just make out the shape of the dam. It was the first warm night. Summer was inching its way in. The water gurgled as it brushed shore. He could hear a train far off, the clacking sound of the rails.

He did an inventory:

He was 35 days back in the world.

In country was a fading idea, concept.

Time had been slow at first.

But gradually it had sped up.

Each day when he looked at woods he saw less jungle.

A car's backfire could still spook him, though.

He missed a few men.

Buddies.

But he knew it was likely he would see none of them again.

And some would never come home.

It was a trifle.

Was it?

Some days, yes.

Some days, no.

Don't mean nothin'.

That's what troopers said.

It wasn't true.

They were just words.

Still, they meant something alright.

Everything.

But he did know, too, why they meant nothing as well.

So.

Well.

The road had gone from pavement to dirt and back to pavement.

Shake it off.

Look ahead.

Don't look back.

A song came to him:

I dreamed I saw the bomber death planes riding shotgun in the sky,

Turning into butterflies above our nation.

31.

Jesse

Jesse found Raul still sitting by the lake and gave him another PBR.

"Thanks, man," Raul said. "Where's Nicole?"

Jesse wedged himself between two boulders and sipped his own beer. He could still picture Nicole clearly, waving and smiling when she turned her VW around and drove slowly down the lane. He'd watched her taillights cross the causeway until they disappeared.

"Gone. About five minutes ago. Said she has an early morning."

"Thought I heard a VW engine," Raul said. "You buy that stuff about going to bed early?"

"Why not?" Jesse lit a joint, inhaled, and passed it. He'd expected a remark about Nicole. He figured to just dodge it. He had learned that sometimes Raul just fired things off wildly.

"Is that the first thing you do every morning, Jesse — roll a doobie and slip it in a pocket for later?"

"No. The first thing I do is piss and wait for my eyes to open, then I roll a doobie to smoke. Then I roll one for later. Used to, anyway.

"Used to?"

"Thinking real serious about quitting, Raul. Real serious. Serious as a grave digger."

"Bullshit."

"No, for real, man." Jesse knew Raul would doubt him. "This is the last one until after we do the deal tomorrow. That's a start."

"I suppose so," Raul said. "A baby step."

"A step's a step," Jesse said.

Raul lightly punched Jesse's arm. "Thought you said you might get in her pants. That's why I left, man. I even figured to sleep under the trees tonight. It's a nice warm night."

"It is," Jesse said absently after picturing Nicole for a moment.

They watched a jon boat with a tiny light mounted on the outboard cross the lake and enter a cove. The man was just a shadowy lump rising above the boat, but they could see his arm on the throttle handlebar behind him.

"That old boy's running trot lines for catfish," Jesse said. "I've seen him before."

"Maybe he'll catch something," Raul said. "But you came up empty. You came up gripping your joint by yourself."

Jesse laughed, knew Raul's tone was friendly.

"She said a cookout's not a date."

"No shit? Sure seems like one to me."

"It's a semi-date," Jesse said. "Because there's food involved, it's a semi-date."

Raul finished the last of his beer.

"That's two cookouts, bro." he said. "Don't two cookouts add up to a full date?"

"Nope. But she said it was a nice try."

"At least you asked. But why don't they add up? Women can be weird alright."

"Tell me about it," Jesse said. "She said if I had picked her up and we'd gone someplace else after dinner, then it would have been a date."

"And met her parents."

"Right."

"So after two cookouts you're still in the hole," Raul said. "Not hers, though."

"Takes two dates for that. Two full dates — then it's negotiable."

"How do you know that?"

"She explained it. She's very specific, that Nicole. Very specific. Has her own way of looking at stuff, for sure."

The joint had become a fading ember between Raul's thumb and forefinger. "You want to roach it?"

"Naw. I'm quitting, remember?"

"That's right, Jesse. You're a changed man now."

"Maybe I am." Jesse felt he was in some ways — felt rather than knew that he could explain it. And he sensed there were changes to come he did not even know about. What was that saying? We don't know yet what we don't know. That was a good one.

"Change is pretty slow," Raul said. "It can be like a glacier. Believe me, I know."

"For sure," Jesse said. He was wondering what it would really require of him to stop smoking weed.

"Jesse, don't she even give you credit for two cookouts? You spent money. That should count."

"It does — half a date. The two add up to a half. She said if we go have a pizza and I pick her up, that's date number one. See what I'm up against?"

"She's making you work for it, bro. Without a doubt."

"It's worth it — she's worth it," Jesse said, but he was a little leery of seeming too much like a syrupy dope to Raul.

"She's a smart girl, Jesse."

"I know it."

"Do you?"

"Yeah. I do." Jesse wondered what was unsaid. Raul was pretty frustrating when he was like that. "What are you driving at?"

"It's not my business," Raul said. "I shouldn't have said anything."

"But you did, so what the fuck do you mean?" Jesse was surprised at his own tone.

Raul picked up a rock and tossed it with a loud plop into the lake. "I didn't mean anything by it, Jesse."

"You meant something."

Raul threw another rock.

"She's got a plan, Jesse. That's all I meant. This stuff about what makes a date, that's setting standards. She looks far down a road. I just was saying I don't know if you look as far as she does. But it's not my business."

They watched as the fisherman's boat reappeared and hugged the shore until it reached another cove and disappeared again.

"How many trot lines does that guy have?" Raul said.

"He runs them all the way from up here to the dam," Jesse said. "Four coves. Last week I watched him hit all four, then cross the lake again for home."

"He's a methodical bastard," Raul said.

"I guess that's because he has a plan."

"There you go," Raul said. "Do you, Jesse?"

"I told you mine the other day, man. After this deal I'm getting out."

"And maybe going to college."

"Maybe. But getting out, that'd be a good first step. That would be solid, Raul."

"You see that, do you?"

"I do. So what the fuck's your plan, man?"

Raul threw another rock into the lake. "To not get arrested, maimed, or killed during this drug deal tomorrow."

Jesse threw a rock, too. "That's a pretty good plan."

32.

Jesse

What did she really know about Jesse? What did she need to know? She had to concede to herself that what she felt to be considerable powers of deduction and intuition could sometimes be less effective when they concerned someone she liked. Overall she was better at assessing strangers because she could be more objective — more scientific.

Take Dom, for instance. Mysterious, sometimes, but no real mystery. Not unfathomable. He was probably a bit of a hotshot coming out of high school in Argus and going into the Army. One of those guys she remembered for their locker room boasting and smug self-confidence flirting with girls in the halls. Then he went to Vietnam and saw a much wider, more dangerous world, and it shocked him some, took the edge off that cockiness in a hurry, and made him question things more than he ever had. He would need something to boost his confidence, something to build on to shed all the self-doubt and fear. A girlfriend would be a good start, she thought, and perhaps she should devote some effort to looking into that. She would give some thought to whether there was someone she knew who would be suitable for him. But someone strong. No prissy maids. Dom would be a handful, at first, for almost any woman.

She would look into it.

Then there was the Chief. He was an altogether different deal than either Dom or Jesse. The Chief was a grown man of 40, a cop, a man trained to deal with very bad people — like her, a psychologist of sorts who relied on their ability to size people up. He was a handsome man, and if he was younger or she was older — maybe. Maybe not. She had heard that he was meeting women discreetly in the local churches. People introduced him to friends. He made his appearances at places like Bunnie's and was happy to be introduced to people, to women. He was a good catch by Argus standards. The Chief, she knew, was not likely interested in a girlfriend. Not for long, anyway. He would be careful about his entanglements. No doubt he'd had plenty of those in Chicago. No, he was probably in the market for a wife, someone he could quickly get past the bullshit of dating with and settle into something. Just what was hard to say. Nicole did not know what sort of husband he might make, but her intuition said he would likely be decent at it, but have his days when he would seem wishy-washy — no, that was perhaps not the right terminology: days when he would be off someplace in his head and his wife would have the challenge of understanding that was just part of who he was, or to spin her wheels trying to do something about it.

Nicole was certain that the Chief was a pretty complicated man. She had recognized in him that professional ability to abruptly observe the etiquette of a situation while reeling himself in from someplace far off mentally. That was something of a gift and demonstrated intelligence, she knew. Like anyone, he had his fair share of self-doubt, but could manage it better than someone like Dom or Jesse. His job demanded that he could downshift quickly and file away troubles for later. She admired that about him. And he seemed to be handling Jesse with a light touch, with some room for maneuver.

Jesse. She felt he was still more of a boy than a man, but he had potential. She knew that she had much to learn, too, but she was willing — eager — to learn it, to get started. Jesse seemed to share that belief, too. Together they might make something stronger than just the sum of themselves and she was willing to try the experiment.

But pragmatic enough to know she should have a Plan B.

33.

Art

Sunday morning, Art had been tempted to go to the early Mass just to steal a look at Carolyn, but decided he would wait until after to meet her for coffee at Cameron's. It wouldn't do to look too eager. She was a teacher after all, and so pretty smart and she would likely sense over-eagerness. Instead, he put on sweats and took a brisk walk through the neighborhood, even running a few yards here and there, but discovered his legs weren't in running shape and perhaps swimming at the school pool was still his best bet. He showered and selected his best — newest — blue Oxford shirt and gray slacks — gray was more formal than khaki, of course, and this was his first date with Carolyn. He thought in the mirror he even looked a little professorial, though for that he knew he would need longer hair. If he let his hair grow just a little more people would notice, but he didn't really think they'd care. He was the Chief, after all. He knew that no one seemed to care that he didn't wear ties. A little more hair wouldn't hurt anything at all. Just to his collar, though. Much beyond that might be too much. Sideburns? No, he didn't like them. They were pretty popular, some inching down to a man's jawbone, but they weren't for Art. They were too blatant. And he worried that sideburns would make him appear to be like one of those dicey redneck sheriffs people thought of in places like Mississippi or Alabama.

He ate a hearty breakfast of eggs and sausage links as well as patties, toast with butter and strawberry jam and some honey, too. No coffee. He didn't want to tank up because he didn't know how much he might drink with Carolyn. He figured he should eat well because it was a late morning coffee date and he didn't know whether that meant lunch, too, or just coffee. It could go either way and it always seemed like a man never knew how it would go until it did. He didn't know if she would want lunch, for example, because maybe that was too much at first. He would be happy to buy lunch. But maybe coffee was as far as she felt comfortable with at first. Art knew he had to gauge all that and figure out where things were going as they unfolded and he just didn't think he was very good at that.

As he drove to Cameron's he took stock of what he knew about Carolyn and why he had been attracted to her: she was pretty, of course, and she resembled an actress — Julie Newmar, he thought. It took a minute to come up with the name. Carolyn had a very nice figure from what he could see at church, which wasn't much. He liked how she listened. Not just to him, but others, too. He had watched her, studied her some from a distance at church as she gabbed with others. She had a way of shifting her weight from one leg to another that seemed to Art to be a sign she weighed things carefully, though he knew it could also just mean she was restless. If she was, she hid it well because when people spoke to her she kept eye contact and nodded her head — sometimes rubbing her chin thoughtfully. Art liked that. It was a nice touch.

Attraction was a funny thing to Art. He didn't understand it and maybe it was something that really couldn't be understood. It just was or it wasn't. Chemistry was a big part of it. Was it really as simple as how someone smelled? It seemed so to him sometimes. Some women really liked him and some not at all and he wondered but never really knew why that was so. In Chicago he had heard it explained by a college professor in a tavern. Genetics, the man said. It was all in genetics. Women back in prehistoric days aligned themselves with good hunters, providers. It was all pretty much practical considerations back then. People had evolved remarkably since then, the professor had said, though Art felt that in the area of violence people hadn't evolved all that much. If anything, the art of killing and taking from others had evolved from primitive basics to high art and science. The human race had not improved in that area of evolution. Vietnam, like his Korea, was just the latest installment. No shortage of violence in the world. He only had to run a finger along the little scar on his cheek where the bullet had nipped at him to know that. As for women, the professor had told him seriously, though perhaps also a little drunkenly, that they had evolved remarkably, of course, but it was still in their genes to gravitate toward good providers.

How did women detect a good provider at first? Art mulled that as he parked and then walked casually toward Cameron's. Is that where chemistry — smell — came into play? And what role did cologne or aftershave play in that? Could those things actually skew the process? He had declined to splash either on that morning in case it was better not to at first. What he normally used — English Leather — wasn't expensive and maybe she would notice that and so he was pleased he avoided it.

Art arrived first and ducked into the men's room to check himself in the mirror. He thought he looked pretty presentable. He cleaned up pretty well, as the saying went.

He studied his hair. Yes, he just might let it grow some more. He thought momentarily of Jesse's long and curly blonde hair. Rock star hair. He couldn't imagine himself like that, but all in all long hair did not bother him one bit. It was merely a personal choice. He had thick brown hair with a good clean part on the left. It was almost to his collar and another inch might be just about right. He imagined that would make him even seem a couple years younger. When he came out of the men's room, he saw Carolyn coming through the café's door. She didn't seem to notice him and he studied her a moment as she looked for a place to sit. He knew that some women felt very self-conscious entering a public place alone, but he didn't think Carolyn seemed that way. She said hello to several people she knew and then slid into a booth near the door. He went over to the booth and she smiled as he approached and sat down.

"Good timing," Carolyn said. "I just sat down."

"It is good timing." Art stopped himself from explaining he went to the bathroom first. He knew the small talk at first between a man and a woman was always stilted, repetitive. The waitress bailed him out temporarily by taking their coffee order. The next step was obvious to him:

"How are you, Carolyn?" The empty salutation was expected, but he didn't imagine so very much could have changed in less than a day.

"Fine," she said. "Very well. Church was inspiring. The Father talked about hope."

"He's good at that," Art said, immediately hoping it didn't sound sarcastic. He was just trying to follow the script as he understood it. He figured if she mentioned he should have been there to hear it, that could be an admonishment, but she didn't say anything more about the homily.

"You're not Catholic, Art, are you?"

"No, I'm not." He didn't think her tone was judgmental. "I'm not sure what I am."

Carolyn chuckled and smiled broadly and Art knew that was a good sign. He sipped his coffee and thought the ice was broken fairly well.

"The Father said you were just keeping tabs on us," she said. "But he was just kidding, of course."

"He can be a kidder alright," Art said. "I've noticed that in him."

"Yes, but in a way it's true, isn't it? I mean, you're the chief of police. I've heard you visit all the churches."

"Where'd you hear that?"

"People talk. It's a small enough town. Not like your Chicago."

"Chicago isn't mine anymore. It was repossessed some time ago."

She laughed heartily at the remark, even throwing her head back some and exposing her neck more. Her skin was white but not too pale, and smooth. She struck him as perceptive and not afraid to speak her mind and he liked that. He did not merely want an admirer. A cooperative partner was more like it.

"You've been to all the churches, Art?"

"Every one I know of. Part of the duty. Or maybe I just like churches."

"Do you?"

"I like the architecture and the trappings."

"What about the messages?"

"I keep my ears open, Carolyn. I think I'm open-minded."

"That's good, Art. I think there are people who wonder that about policemen."

He wondered if that was a challenge of some sort. "We're not so different from anyone else." He shrugged in hopes of trivializing it, disposing of it. She didn't say anything more about it, but kept a wry smile, and the silence intimidated Art a little.

She stirred a few drops of cream into her coffee.

"Which church is your favorite, Art?"

Most interesting, or most comfortable, he thought. "Father Malinowski keeps a good church. All of them are very nice, though."

Always be diplomatic. Cultivate the proper public image. He stopped himself from saying the Baptists made him a little nervous with their strident views. He was thankful there was no Mormon church. He had grave reservations about that and was glad he would not have to deal with it. Pentecostal, too, troubled him. That church was small, on the outskirts of Argus toward Bloomington and away from the lake. The people there had been welcoming and friendly, but very narrow. Too narrow for Art.

"They all want the Chief to favor them, I imagine," she said. "I certainly understand that."

"The Chief is retired today. I'm just Art."

Carolyn's eyebrows rose slightly, but the Chief was sure she appreciated his attempt at being casual.

"Have you been to the little church out in the country?" she said. "Just the other side of Kelton, beyond the lake. I don't know anything about it, though."

"Out of my jurisdiction," Art said. He had been to Kelton, but not beyond and did not know of the church.

"I suppose so," she said. "But what if they do strange things out there? What if they do all that snake-handling crap? You've heard of all that?"

He thought that was a strange thing to bring up out of the blue, but was getting used to how straightforward Carolyn could be.

"I've heard of that stuff. Sure. Down south, though, isn't it? I mean south like in the real south. The Carolinas, Georgia maybe. Not southern Illinois."

"Southern Illinois can be pretty squirrelly, Art. Have you been there?"

"No. Argus is as far as I've been. Should I go for a visit?"

"It's lovely country down there," she said. "Hills and forests like you don't quite get here. But more like the real south than around here. Much more. Being from Chicago, you might feel you'd gone much further than you realized down there."

He wasn't sure why she went on about it. "Have you been to Chicago, Carolyn?"

"Goodness, yes. I guess about a dozen times. Maybe more. I have a sister in Evanston. I've been to Wrigley Field. And Soldier Field, too. I love Michigan Avenue, and the lake."

"Evanston's nice," Art said. "I lived south of there, in Rogers Park."

"My sister loves it there. She loves the city and the fast pace."

"But that's not for you?"

"Not really. Too fast, I think. I really like visiting, but I'm always happy to get back here, back home. I grew up here. My family goes back to the town's founding. This is home."

Art admired that sense of history and community that came so easy to her. It made him acutely aware that he was a transplanted outsider. But he hoped very much to think of Argus as his home in the same way Carolyn did.

"Did you get your teaching degree at ISU, Carolyn?"

"No, I went over to Champaign, to U of I. In those days I wanted to be a little further from here than just Bloomington. Now that I look back on it, it was only a few miles in the other direction. But back then it seemed far more. Isn't that funny?"

"It is. I think the world seems bigger when you're a kid, but gets smaller each year you live."

"Until it shrinks to the size of a postage stamp?" She kept a straight face just long enough to make him wonder if she was really serious before letting the smile flash again. He was learning that she could be quite the kidder, quite the live wire with an odd but entertaining way of looking at things. He felt they might be compatible, but one just never knew about those things. As a cop he felt he was pretty good at detecting sincerity in people, but that ability diminished when applied to his personal life because then emotion became a factor, and desire. Those things were cut out of the equation when he was a cop sizing up someone.

"I suppose Argus could feel a little small sometimes," Art said. "Limited."

"But if it's really home, then it doesn't feel limited. It feels just right. Do you think it's limiting, Art?"

He did not. After Chicago, he actually felt it was liberating, roomy. "No. No, I don't. I like the space, the elbow room. The slower pace, too. And the lake."

"But you had Lake Michigan in Chicago. I'm always amazed at how far across it is."

"But only the rich can live by it," Art said. "That's different here."

"Do you admire the rich, Art?"

"No, I don't think so. I get a kick out of their houses, though. How's that?"

Art elected not to tell her that he was vaguely suspicious of very rich people. He had seen too many people make money in Chicago from what he called corner-cutting. Corner-cutters were people who weren't always honest or ethical and who would step on people to get ahead. They cheated on their taxes and cheated people routinely in deals. He enjoyed touring the middle class area of Lake Argus, for example, but never felt quite comfortable in that wealthy enclave on the peninsula with its faux mansions. Those people shopped for groceries in Argus because it was close, but otherwise maintained distant lives from the rest and socialized in Bloomington.

"That's right," Carolyn said. "You like to study the architecture of churches, so why not houses, too. Did you ever want to be an architect?"

Art did not think that had ever really crossed his mind. "I think my interest in architecture is sort of new. I didn't think much about those things when I was younger. Did you always want to be a teacher, Carolyn?"

"Yes. Since maybe grade school I wanted to be a teacher. But you're changing the subject. We were trying to find out who you are."

"I'm no mystery," he said, knowing full well it wasn't true, but wanting to appear as uncomplicated to Carolyn as possible. He felt that women did not want men who were complicated, that it might even be perceived as a sign of weakness. Was that somehow connected to what the professor had told him about how men and women evolve?

"Oh, I don't know about that," she said. "I think there's more to you than meets the eye, Art."

"No, no," he protested, and he looked out a window a moment. "I'm an open book. Just ask me something and I'll tell you what I think."

"OK," she said. "Do you want to have lunch?"

"Lunch?" Art wasn't prepared for the sudden shift in direction because he was concentrating too hard on appearing uncomplicated.

"You said to just ask something, so I'm asking," Carolyn said.

Art reached for a menu. "Of course. Yes. Lunch. I'd love to."

"But not here," she said. "Cameron's is more of a breakfast place, don't you think? I know a nice place over in Bloomington. Interested?"

Art fumbled to slip the folder back into its holder. "Sure. Yeah, Bloomington's fine. You're right — Cameron's sort of tails off after breakfast. Bloomington's better. Much better."

"You didn't have any plans, did you, Art? Anything going on today?"

"Not a thing. It's just another quiet Sunday."

34.

Jesse

They had a few hours to kill and went to the little café on the road to Argus from the lake and ate the famous potatoes.

"All the times I've stopped here and I never tried these potatoes," Jesse said. "Pretty damn good."

"The Chief swears by them," Raul said. "It's his religion, I think."

"They're awesome alright. But I don't think the Chief worships them, Raul."

"Not like you worshipped dope."

Jesse knew from Raul's tone it was good-natured. He was getting used to Raul being one of those guys who liked to jerk people around a little just to get a rise out of them.

"Past tense," Jesse said. "As in water under the bridge and way downstream."

"After today, that is," Raul said. "You won't be a changed man until after today."

Jesse allowed the logistics of the impending deal to flash across his mind. "Actually, not for a week, Raul. There's distribution to do. Then maybe I call myself a changed man."

"That's right. After all, it's a business." Raul pushed his empty plate away. "Are you nervous, Jesse?"

Jesse was indeed nervous, but also feeling regret. He wished he could walk away from it all immediately. The past year had begun to make him feel a little soiled. He had stayed awake very late the night before and slept fitfully, finally awaking with the firm belief he really was in the throes of a transition — but to what? College was the standard answer, and he believed that was a step. But it remained rather vague. So did Nicole. He wasn't sure yet what it all added up to.

"Nervous? Yeah, some. I wish it was over."

"We still have an hour to kill." Raul glanced at his watch. "Are you OK?"

"I don't know." Jesse got up. "I need to move around. Stretch my legs."

"Sure, man."

Jesse knew Raul was looking at him with some puzzlement. They paid at the register and went outside into the sunshine. Jesse walked past the GTO, out near the road, and looked up it toward town before walking back to Raul, who waited patiently in front of the car.

"What if we just skipped it?" Jesse said. "Just not show up. What do you think?"

Raul blinked several times, but didn't say anything. He stared at Jesse.

"We could do that," Jesse said. "We could just –"

"Jesus fucking Christ, Jesse. Hell of a time to bring it up." Raul looked again at his watch. "Just blow it off? Just like that?"

"Yeah. Just do something else — go fishing."

"Fishing?" Raul sagged against the GTO. "Just pretend it doesn't exist, didn't happen? That sort of shit?"

Jesse was skeptical, too. "Won't work?"

"I don't think so, Jesse. You made a deal. This fuckhead Brant is coming — like in about thirty or forty minutes. He might be there already, waiting."

"I know." Jesse took a few steps away from the car, looking at the ground with his hands deep in his jeans' pockets. He turned back to Raul. "But what if I show up and explain I'm out, that I can't do it anymore? I show up and take responsibility for it, but I bow out, respectfully."

Raul frowned. "This ain't like a political race, Jesse, where you shake hands with your opponent, wish them luck, and just move on."

"No, I suppose it ain't."

"And he's obviously come from a long ways off."

"I could give him money," Jesse said. "He would probably understand that."

"He's a freaking drug lord, Jesse. You don't know what he might be capable of. I saw some of that shit in the Nam. People get killed pretty fucking easy in that business."

Jesse smirked. "You make him sound like Al Capone, man."

"Well, fuck, man — he sort of is Al Capone."

Jesse felt that was an exaggeration, fueled partly by whatever was fueling Raul's anger — coming home from Nam, feeling lost, whatever.

"He's just a businessman, Raul. He's motivated by money. I know some people in Bloomington I can maybe connect him with. Redirect the deal, man. He might respond to that. What does he care whether it's me or them as long as he does business?"

"You're guessing he'll be reasonable about it," Raul said. "We don't know that. What if he makes a fuss about it?"

"What can he do about it? He can't make me sell dope."

"I don't know what he might do, Jesse. That's the part that bothers me."

"Bunnie's is a public place. He won't want publicity. He can't afford trouble."

"If he's smart and sane, you mean. We don't know what he can afford."

Jesse looked out over the cornfields a moment. "Well, either way, I guess you're right. I have to go meet him. I realize that. You're right about that. I got myself in it and I have to get myself out."

"Being right doesn't make me feel any better, Jesse."

"I hear you." Jesse thought about it a moment longer. "Don't go, Raul, if that's how you feel. I have to, but you don't."

"What are you going to tell him?"

"The truth. I don't want to deal dope anymore. I don't want to do this last deal. He'll just have to accept it. I won't run. I think that's sort of what I've been doing living out in this trailer — running from something. Time to stop. I'll show up because I said I would. But it's time I did the right thing and moved on. That's the way it is."

He exchanged glances with Raul and hoped he appeared resolute. He felt queasy inside, but strangely hopeful, too.

"OK, Jesse. I'll go with you."

"It's OK if you don't, Raul. I'd understand."

"No you wouldn't. You'd be pissy about it." But Raul smiled softly. "Someone has to watch your back, kid."

"I'm not a kid anymore. Not after today."

Raul nodded. "I think that's about right. Sorry. You're no kid. You're sounding like a man."

"I'm doing the right thing, Raul. It's the hard thing, but it's the right thing."

"I think so, too, Jesse."

"Doesn't make it any easier, though, does it?"

"Not one fucking bit."

They took the long way around the lake into town to give themselves time to think it all through. It was a quiet ride, no music, no joints, just the squeaky sound of the tires on asphalt and steady growl of the GTO's engine. Jesse felt surprisingly calm at that point, figuring he had made his decision and in doing so some of the weight had come off. They would just go to Bunnie's, no dilly-dallying, no farting around and debating it further — just find this dickhead Brant and explain politely but firmly that things had changed for him and he no longer could be part of something he didn't believe in anymore. Was it really something like that, something a person could believe in? It was just drug commerce. Pretty sorry-ass and greedy shit at that. Would this Brant be offended if he said he didn't believe in doing it anymore? Too bad if he was, Jesse decided. Maybe it had to be said in order to make the change have real meaning.

Jesse looked over at Raul a couple times. Mostly Raul looked out his window at the passing cornfields. Jesse could guess his thoughts: what was ahead, how would it play out, what were the dangers. Stuff like that. Raul probably approached it like another military mission, like being back in Vietnam, maybe. Jesse was glad Raul was along to ride shotgun.

They pulled into Bunnie's lot and the crunching of gravel beneath the tires seemed louder to Jesse than usual. They quickly saw the blue Econoline van, parked in a corner of the lot and Jesse wheeled the GTO over, but there was no one inside that they could see. They sat there a minute, the nose of the GTO pointed directly at the front of the van, not quite sure of the next move.

"We're too exposed here," Raul said. "That's not good. He must be inside Bunnie's. We have to go find him."

"Roger," Jesse said, immediately thinking it sounded too military. They got out and stood next to the GTO a few seconds, then Raul gingerly eased over to the van and looked through the windshield, cupping his hands over his eyes.

"Nope," he said. Jesse nodded and they started across the lot, more gravel crunching beneath their shoes.

"He said he would know us," Jesse said.

"That's what you said the other day. Because he's God, man. The god of drugs."

Jesse abruptly halted and looked around.

"What's wrong, Jesse?"

"The Chief. I was just wondering if he was around somewhere."

Raul looked around, too. "No way. He's somewhere else. Doing whatever he does on a Sunday."

"Maybe he's out eating the famous potatoes."

"I'm surprised we didn't see him there," Raul said.

When they reached the door, Jesse grabbed the handle and then as quickly released it.

"Here's how I figure it, Raul. No idling. We walk in, locate him, and go straight over and I tell him straight out. I think it has to be done quick."

"Makes sense." Raul nodded, mulled it a few seconds. "But you can't spook him. You hear what I'm saying? You can't just hit and run."

"You want to have lunch with him, Raul? Drink some beers — maybe plug the juke box and chat about the Cubs?"

"That's not what I'm saying, Jesse. But it has to be diplomatic. We need to be able to walk out of this place and never see this fuck again. It all needs to end right here."

"OK. I hear you."

"You do?"

"Yeah. We could get a couple beers at the bar, then go over."

"What if he's sitting at the bar? What if he recognizes us before we can do that? Are you ready for that?"

Jesse put his hand back on the door handle. "I don't think he'll sit at the bar, Raul. I know a few thing about this business. He'll want one of the booths, one that's out of the flow of traffic with a little privacy. Even if he sat at the bar — and I don't think so — he'd take a stool down at the far end, with his back to the wall, where he can watch who comes in and size them up. But he'll take one of those booths with a clear view of the door and sit facing us."

Raul nodded. "That sounds right. He'll wave us over?"

"He knows I have long blonde hair and that there's two of us. He'll give some subtle sign of recognition. He'll expect me to know it. Then we go over."

"Damn," Raul said. "This is like being in the fucking CIA."

"Pretty much, man. OK. So, we go in and immediately go to the bar and get beers. That will give me time to glance around and find him. We sit down and I tell him nice, but straight out. We don't even have to finish the beers. They're just props, man. We leave them when it's done and that's that. Ready?"

"Fire away."

"Don't say that."

Inside it took a few seconds for their eyes to adjust. The bar was right there by the door and the bartender was, too. They got two Budweisers and Jesse leaned an elbow on the bar, chugged a good amount of his beer, and looked around. Their guy was right where Jesse expected him to be, in a far booth with a clear view of the entire bar and the door.

Jesse had expected a longhair, but the man's hair was only a few inches past his collar with a center part, and he had a thick, dark moustache. Oddly enough, he vaguely reminded Jesse of Groucho Marx. Details, Jesse thought. Details. The man — Brant — wore a lightweight blue jacket, one of those flimsy ones that could barely hold out a breeze, over a t-shirt. He had a small canvas shoulder bag on the table. If there was dope in the bag the guy was a fool, Jesse thought. He didn't think this Brant had come across like a fool on the phone. Brant was still too far away in the poor light for Jesse to know his age, but he sensed he was well over thirty.

Brant nodded almost reluctantly, but it was enough for Jesse to recognize.

He turned back to Raul. "That's our guy. Far booth."

"Ready, Jesse?"

"Yeah. If we hesitate too long he'll be suspicious."

They both took gulps of their beer and went over.

"You're Jesse," Brant said and it wasn't a question.

"Yeah. This is Raul. He jut got back from Vietnam." Jesse immediately wondered why he said that. Out of the corner of his eye he saw Raul suppress a frown.

"He's the partner you mentioned?" Brant said. Brant looked Raul over carefully. "Have a seat, boys."

"I'm not his partner," Raul said as he slid into the booth after Jesse. "Just a friend."

"Along for the ride," Brant said.

"Something like that."

Jesse gauged Brant's face and recognized the man was suddenly wary of Raul.

Brant shifted his glance to Jesse. "You need a bodyguard?"

Jesse grinned broadly, attempted disarmament. "No, no. Not at all. He's a friend. Just another set of eyes and ears, man. It's OK. Really."

"You said he was back from Vietnam. Was that some sort of message — warning?"

Jesse had a good sense already of what type of dealer Brant was: not a good one. Not a very reasonable one. The guy had a quick temper.

"It's what it is," Raul said and Jesse knew that was indeed a warning. Subtle, but a warning. Things weren't starting off well at all.

"It's cool, man," Jesse said decisively, firmly.

"It better be," Brant said as he stared at Raul.

"No need to sweat, man," Jesse said. "The thing is, I'm here to tell you I can't do the deal." The way things were going Jesse knew he had to just get it on the table fast. The possibility of a quick hit and departure had evaporated. It would be hard to get out now.

Brant's eyes darted back to Jesse. He studied Jesse's face and his own face darkened a little.

"Say what?"

"I'm getting out of the business, man." Jesse tried to smile again but was too nervous to do it well. He hoped it didn't come out a frown. "I'm sorry you had to come so far. I had no way to get a hold of you. I do apologize for that."

Jesse wished he could see Raul's face, but he dared not break eye contact with Brant, who leaned back against the wall of the booth and let his hands slip from the table onto his lap. Brant sighed and stared at Jesse.

"I drove a long fucking way, man. Two hundred freaking miles. And now you show up to say thanks but no thanks?"

"I think that's what he's telling you, ace," Raul said and Jesse saw anger in Brant's eyes.

It's all on the table finally, Jesse thought. He wished he could feel good about it.

"If I could have gotten a hold of you, I would have," Jesse said. "I just made the decision. I'm real sorry, man. But

I can make it up to you. I know some guys in Bloomington. I can put you with them. They know their shit. You won't lose anything on this deal. You'll still come out. Believe me, it ain't a wasted trip."

Brant briefly looked toward the door then back to Jesse. "No, it ain't going to be a wasted trip. That's for fucking sure."

"Great," Jesse said, hoping that meant Brant could still be reasonable. He wanted desperately to see what was on Raul's face. Brant kept track of both of them.

"You can make it up to me alright," Brant said. "You just take the fucking product I drove two hundred freaking miles to sell you and you call your buddies in Bloomington and you sell it, smoke it — shove it up your ass for all I care."

Not good, Jesse thought. Not at all. He allowed himself a quick glance at Raul, who kept his eyes on Brant. Those two could tangle pretty damn quickly. He had to head that off.

"The thing is, Brant, I'm not sure you catch my drift entirely. I'm not a connection any more. But the good news? I can grease the deal for you with some others — and they're cool, man, believe me — and you're set. See? Bingo, man. You just get someone else's money, but it's just as green as anybody else's."

Brant shook his head. "You don't palm me off on people I don't know ahead of time. That ain't how it works, mister no-longer-a-connection. What, you got a conscience all of a sudden? Got religion? What?"

"Time to move on," Jesse said. "That's all. I guess I wasn't cut out for this business after all. Thinking of going back to college."

"How sweet," Brant said. "And you brought your soldier buddy to what, try and scare me?"

"How about I pound your ass right here in this booth?" Raul said quietly.

Brant smiled. "So you're the bodyguard after all." He pulled his jacket open and Raul and Jesse saw a .38 revolver tucked into Brant's jeans. "How about I shoot you in the fucking leg right here in this booth, tough guy? Maybe pop off your kneecap. You think Vietnam's the only dangerous place to be?"

Jesse looked at Raul. His expression was still defiant.

"Listen up, chuckleheads," Brant said. "This is how it goes down. We walk out the fucking door and you give me the fucking money, and maybe I'll even give you the fucking product. Maybe I won't. If you piss me off anymore, I'll leave you high and dry."

Brant pulled out the revolver and pointed it at them under the table.

"Easy," Jesse said. "It's OK, man. Really. There's no need for this."

"There wouldn't be if you had come to live up to the deal, man," Brant said. "The deal goes through. Whether or not you keep anything to sell depends on the next minute or so."

"Let's go, Jesse," Raul said.

"That's better, big boy." Brant tucked the gun back in his jeans and the three of them slid out of the booth and walked slowly to the door. The bartender smiled and half saluted and Brant returned the salute. Had Jesse looked closely, he would have noticed that Raul closed his eyes the last few feet to the door and then on out into the increased light. When they cleared the door Raul whirled around sharply and through blinking eyes Jesse saw Raul and Brant suddenly become a swirl of color punctuated by the loud pop of the revolver going off.

35.

Art

Art was telling Carolyn a story he hoped was funny when he glanced left as they passed Bunnie's and he heard the shot and saw Raul go down. He didn't know it was Raul at first as he wheeled the police cruiser hard left into the tavern's parking lot and instinctively yelled for Carolyn to get down below the dashboard as he forced her down roughly with his right hand. A man in a blue jacket scampered to his feet and picked up a gun as Art popped the glove box and retrieved his own revolver. Then he saw that it was Jesse and Raul, but it was a fleeting recognition as he punched the accelerator and cut the man off from a van he was running toward. The cruiser fishtailed and spewed gravel at the man. There was a tree-lined creek behind Bunnie's and the man hesitated, then ran toward it. Art radioed for help, told Carolyn to go check Raul, and got out and walked cautiously toward the creek. Damn lucky the man didn't put a few through the windshield, Art thought. That night in the alley in Chicago years before flashed across his mind and he hesitated for a moment, too. Up ahead, he thought he saw a flash of blue in the trees. Was it the man or his mind playing tricks? With great effort he regained control and moved toward the creek.

"Be careful, Art," Carolyn called after him and he was momentarily struck by how calm she sounded. His own pulse raced and his mouth was dry.

"See to the boy," he yelled as he quickened his pace toward the creek. He reached the first trees and put a thick trunk between himself and the creek and scanned the area. The creek was only a few feet across and the man could easily be in the trees opposite him, up a short bank. He didn't see anything, didn't hear anything but birds rustling in trees above him. He looked for tracks and saw none. He felt as though he could hear his heart beating. He glanced quickly behind him, but there was nothing to see but the back of Bunnie's.

Art listened for sirens, but there weren't any. He knew he should wait for backup, but he also didn't want one of his officers walking into an ambush. After another quick look across the creek he sprinted a few yards to another tree and crouched behind it for a few seconds before carefully peering around the trunk. He spotted some broken milkweed stalks going up the bank to a grove of trees and bushes. But was that really a sign? A deer could have done that. They were known to frequent the creek. Could a large dog have done it? He cleared his throat and looked across the creek again. Nothing. It was too quiet. He thought of Raul for a moment but forced the thought away. No time for it. Focus is essential. This man — who was he? Art almost wished he knew the man's name. He didn't like the possibility of being killed by someone he didn't even know — or killing someone who was a blank slate. What if the shooting was accidental? Didn't matter. Not really. Raul was down and this stranger was running and had a gun. If he used that gun Art would have to kill him. Shoot and ask questions later. That was how it would have to be. Maybe he would regret the answers, maybe not. But if this man fired, Art would kill him. He would try anyway.

The memory of that night in the Chicago alley came back to him again and in his head he again saw the muzzle flash and felt the sting of the grazing bullet. It came to him in slow motion. He sweated and his forehead itched. He scratched it with the back of a hand and peeked again across the creek. Nothing moved in the grove. There wasn't even a breeze to stir the bushes. He wondered what the man was thinking. What was his plan? He hadn't fired a shot yet. Maybe that was good. Something to build on. Art was thankful there had been no wild gunplay when he pulled into the lot. The man seemed more interested in just getting away. But he had shot Raul. Art didn't know the circumstances. He didn't know shit about the man or anything about why it happened. He was working blind out in the bush. He had a stray thought of Raul in Vietnam, working the bush and trying not to get shot, but looking for someone to shoot — to kill. He wondered if Raul had killed anyone. The Viet Cong. Was that the tick under his skin fueling his drift, his barely-concealed confusion? Or maybe he had killed but didn't know it. Those fire fights could be distant, men dying without their killers ever knowing.

If Art killed today he would know it. It would not be by long distance or anonymous. It would be close, personal. Art did not want to die. He didn't think he would. But you never know, he reminded himself. You just never know. That night in Chicago had been very close indeed. But it wasn't his time. He had been very grateful and prayed with wondrous gratitude in several churches, but after a while the platitudes that came out of the mouths of ministers and priests compelled him to do his praying on his own. Now everything was on the line. His life was connected to a stranger. In a way his life was in this stranger's hands. To a degree, anyway. A lucky shot and there would be no house on Lake Argus. No wife laughing with him under an umbrella by the shore. No boat to motor around the lake in. No house with a big picture window for gazing at the sunset over the lake. No Carolyn. Was Carolyn the one? What an odd thought to have in the middle of a mess. Like his concern for Raul, he forced himself to file Carolyn away. Focus. It's everything. Focus.

He snuck another look across the creek. Where was this bastard? Art believed he was still in the grove across the creek, but which end? Or was he in the middle? But the longer the standoff lasted, the more likely the man would shed his initial fear and indecision and set off down the creek, making him harder to find and a danger to more people. He did wish he knew the man's name, at least. You should at least know something about the man you might kill. Then Art thought about his officers. Any minute he would surely hear a siren. And then he remembered they were all young men, with wives. One had kids. How many? Two. A boy and a girl. Art thought he recalled they were five and two. Too damn young to lose a father. His officers were good men. But they had never seen one of these deals. They had never walked down a dark alley and been surprised by an ugly muzzle flash and felt a bullet tickle their cheeks. They certainly had never killed anyone, or even shot at anyone. All things considered, Art knew he was the most qualified for the task at hand. And he had less to lose than his officers. Did he? What about the house on the lake? What about a wife yet to be? Those were still fantasies. He could not count them.

Art heard a twig snap from across the creek in the small grove of bushes and that told him what he needed to know.

Still there. Thank you very fucking much for being a little predictable. That helps. Then he heard the first siren. Here comes the cavalry. About time. But riding blind, too. They would know almost nothing when they arrived. They would have a man down and Carolyn pointing them in the right direction. That was it. She would tell them he had a gun, but they were good men and would rush to their leader across the open lot behind Bunnie's.

From the grove across the creek the man had a decent field of fire. And he'd already shot one man. Art had to assume he would do it again. It made him lose focus a moment. Was Raul alive? It was tempting to go look. But that would be negligent. And dangerous. He had a duty. It if was bad there wasn't much Art could have done anyway. If it wasn't too bad, Jesse and Carolyn could comfort him as well as anybody. An ambulance would come from Bloomington. But that was twenty-five miles away. A long enough damn time to wait. How long had it already been? He had forgotten to check his watch. His men would have summoned the ambulance. It would be on the way as he crouched behind the tree.

And Raul was a tough kid. If it wasn't too bad he would hold on. He had survived Vietnam. He had seen a lot more war than Art had in Korea. A damn shame, though, if he'd come home just to get shot and killed in his own damn hometown.

To Art's right, on a low-hanging limb, he saw a squirrel. It seemed to be studying him. Art was sure the squirrel was looking right at him. Its tail swished back and forth. It was only a few yards away. That's a good place to be, Art thought — up a tree, out of the line of fire. He wished he was sitting up there, too, alongside that squirrel on the limb, above and detached from what was happening below.

Art swallowed hard, summoned his focus and resolve and glanced again around the tree trunk. He glimpsed a small patch of blue — the man's jacket. Had to be. What else in that grove could be so blue? He picked up a piece of wood at the base of his tree and hefted the revolver in his hand, got a good grip, and with his left hand he tossed the piece of wood toward a tree a few yards away and then wheeled into a crouching firing position and aimed at the grove. Two shots followed the piece of wood and Art fired five at the patch of blue he hoped really was the man's jacket and he heard a high-pitched yelp.

The siren was very loud and very close as Art reloaded. Very good. They're almost here. I may yet need them. But he desperately wanted to resolve it, to end it, before his young men arrived and had to become targets, too. His gun hand shook a bit and he tried to calm himself. He picked up a rock, shifted the revolver to his left hand, and threw the rock into the grove then ducked behind the tree trunk. Nothing happened. He shifted the gun back to his right hand and fired three more shots into the grove and waited again. Nothing. A rush of adrenaline flooded him and propelled him across the creek and up the bank.

He found the man face down, his gun in front of him, and Art held his own gun on the body for a few seconds, but he knew the man was dead. Gut feeling. And there was an exit wound in the back. Art grabbed him by a shoulder and turned him over, the head dangling for a moment grotesquely, and saw another wound in the neck and lots of blood. That was the one that did him. He went fast, probably. That was merciful, Art knew, but he reminded himself that Raul was down. Mercy wasn't part of the equation anymore. The man had not earned mercy. He went through the pocket of the man's jacket quickly and found his wallet. His name was Brant Russell. An Indiana license. So, he had a name. And a home. Art now knew he had killed a real person with a history and not just a complete stranger. He had chased Brant and been shot at by Brant and had killed Brant. And he knew he would live with the memory of Brant a very long time. Who was Brant Russell to Raul? Well, he would find that out soon enough.

Art stared at the body a moment. "You poor dumb son of a bitch. You should have just given up. Maybe this could have all been squared somehow. Maybe it was an accident, what happened to Raul. But you crossed the line and shot at me. I had no choice, Brant."

Art shivered. He felt like crying, came close. But he steeled himself. There was still Raul to see about. There was a canvas bag lying a few feet from the body and Art put its strap across his shoulder, picked up Brant's revolver, and walked toward Bunnie's as two of his officers ran wild-eyed toward him. One of them had forgotten to draw his gun. He would have to speak to him about that.

36.

Raul

He had thought to close his eyes, hoping they would adjust to the light quicker.

It was the edge he needed.

Jesse and Brant the Drug Lord moved in blind slow motion.

It was all clear in his head.

He felt them behind him.

Sensed them.

Clarity.

The most powerful drug of all.

He became a cat.

Maybe a mountain lion.

His turn was quicksilver.

The Drug Lord blinked heavily.

Time stood still.

Raul's hands reached his throat.

They tumbled.

An explosion.

Searing heat in his shoulder.

Jesse yelled something.

Raul collided with the gravel of the parking lot.

More pain.

The world was now ground level looking up.

The Drug Lord ran.

A car skidded in the gravel.

He heard a woman, a stranger: "Be careful, Art."

He heard a familiar voice: "See to the boy."

He tilted his head, now laying flat against the gravel.

He could smell the white dust.

He saw the Drug Lord disappear around a corner of the building.

He saw the Chief hesitate, gun in his hand, then follow.

His last conscious thought: the Chief always gets the last word.

37.

Jesse

The shots made him look up from Raul for a moment. There were two, then five and a pause. Then three more. To Jesse they sounded like firecrackers on the Fourth of July. He was pretty sure Raul had just passed out. He still had a pulse and Jesse knew that was good. But there was a lot of blood from a shoulder wound. The woman with the Chief seemed to have a good head on her shoulders, he thought. She found a first aid kit in the police cruiser and they put a large bandage on the wound and took turns applying pressure. Then the Chief's officers arrived and ran off, too. The woman went to the corner of the building for a look and came back looking relieved.

"I think it's over," she said. " I saw the Chief."

"He's okay?"

"Yes." She took her turn applying pressure. "I'm Carolyn."

"Jesse."

"Who's your friend?"

"Raul — Dominick. Dominick Cruikshank."

"Dom?" She pulled back and looked at his face. "My God. Dominick. I didn't recognize him."

"You know him?"

"I teach at the high school. He was one of my students." She waved Jesse off and resumed her turn on the bandage.

"He's just back from Vietnam," Jesse said, noticing for the first time how bloody his hands were from the bandage.

"That's what I heard," she said. "But I should have recognized him."

Jesse studied Raul's face. "He doesn't really look like himself right now."

She looked, but didn't say anything.

Jesse heard another siren. It sounded far off yet.

"Do you hear it?" he said.

She cocked her head. "Yeah, I hear it."

"More cops?"

"Ambulance, I hope. He needs it."

Jesse looked again at Raul, wondered if his new friend was going to die. He remembered that there would be an awful lot to explain, but he didn't care about anything but helping Raul. Nothing else really mattered.

"Here, my turn," he said and Carolyn eased back on her haunches and started to wipe a strand of hair from her cheek but remembered the blood and stared at her hands a moment.

"It's a lot of blood," Jesse said.

"He's got more. He'll make it. Dom was always pretty resilient."

Jesse thought Carolyn was pretty tough, too.

In a few minutes the Chief and his men came back. The Chief had a look Jesse had never seen on his face before. It seemed like a combination of surprise and fear. He was carrying a gun and Jesse noticed Brant's canvas shoulder bag, too. Details. Jesse was always good at noticing details. Jesse really wanted to know what was in that bag. He figured he'd know soon enough. He wondered if the Chief had already looked. Maybe not. The Chief looked pretty shook up. Was Brant dead? Must be. All that shooting must have hit something. If he wasn't dead, where was he? No, he had to be dead. Jesus. One minute they're talking and the next the guy's dead. The Chief really did look like he'd seen something awful. Did Vietnam sound like that?

"How is he?" the Chief said.

"He's alive, Art," Carolyn said. "His name is Dominick. He was one of my students."

"Yeah, I know him." The Chief looked at the bloody bandage. "Is he hit anywhere else?"

"I don't think so," Jesse said. Then he looked up at the Chief. "Brant?"

"Mr. Russell is dead, Jesse." The Chief looked away.

"I didn't known his last name. Russell."

The Chief started to say something else, but the siren from Bloomington was very loud and then the ambulance pulled into the lot and everyone looked at it except Jesse, who kept applying pressure to the bandage.

38.

Art

He allowed Jesse to ride to Bloomington in the ambulance with Raul. It was a five-star fucking mess, but it would get sorted out. Jesse wasn't going anywhere. It was a clean shooting. Cut and dried. Black and white. Even righteous. It was over and then again it wasn't. That would take time. In Chicago there would be people he could talk to after a shooting. Counseling. Help with the grief and all that. Carolyn drove him home that night and poured him a glass of wine and steered him to his easy chair and she sat on the couch with a glass, too. Nothing was said for several minutes.

"You sure do show a gal a hell of a first date," Carolyn finally said.

He stared a few seconds and then laughed with her and felt a little better. Within an hour one of his men called from the hospital in Bloomington and said Dom was stable and the doctors believed he'd pull through just fine.

"That's wonderful news, Art."

"Yes, it is." He raised his glass to her in a toast. "I already have one body. I don't need two."

"You had no choice, Art."

"That's right." He gulped some of the wine. He knew there was an awful lot she probably wanted to ask. He could talk about it, he felt. But if she didn't ask, that was okay, too.

Carolyn refilled their glasses. "Maybe we should get drunk, Art."

"Maybe so. It wouldn't be the worst thing that happened to me today."

"No, it wouldn't."

After a minute Art said, "Brant Russell."

She nodded.

"He was from Indiana. Terre Haute. He was thirty-five. I did the math off his license."

"And he had a mother and a father, too," Carolyn said. "But he didn't give you a choice, Art."

"Tell that to his mother and father."

"Someone will, unfortunately. Not you, Art. That's not your worry."

"No, my job was just to kill him."

"As harsh as maybe it sounds, yes it was. You knew that when you signed on, Art. But you protected your town. Mr. Russell might have hurt others."

"I did my duty."

"Yes. Yes, you did."

Art knew that was right. But he also knew that you can rationalize things like that all day, but in the end you had killed someone, and when you did, a little piece of you died with them if you had a conscience at all, and having a conscience was one of the things Art was proud of. But it meant absorbing a lot of pain and punishment, too. He suddenly could not imagine what it must have been like on the ground in Korea or Vietnam and having to kill randomly and often and then moving on to do it again. He knew that soldiers got used to it, got hardened to it, but he could not imagine such a transformation. He could not fathom what it must have been like for Dom.

"What was Dom like in high school, Carolyn?"

"He was full of piss and vinegar. But I always felt Dominick could amount to something."

"Yeah, that sounds like him alright."

"How do you know him, Art?"

Art thought back to the day he first saw Dom waiting for Jesse outside Ferguson's IGA. Dom had come out looking a little shaky and leaned against a rack of shopping carts, his eyes closed, the sun warming his face. Art had thought he looked like a man who did better outdoors than indoors and would for a while.

"When he got back from Vietnam he hooked up with Jesse. Dom camped out on the lake, by Jesse's trailer."

"I met Jesse. Who is he?"

Art sipped his wine. "Jesse is a first-class drug dealer, Carolyn."

"I see. Well. So that's what all this is about?"

"That would be my guess," Art said. "I'll find out soon enough."

"A deal gone bad," Carolyn said.

"Seems to fit the circumstances."

"Could it have been an accident? The shooting?"

"I don't think so, Carolyn. It could have been. That's certainly possible. But my gut tells me it wasn't. When I talk to Jesse and Dom, we'll know the answer."

"Where does Dom fit in the picture?"

"I don't know for sure. My guess is he's a spectator with an awful damn good seat. I had a talk with him one day. My sense of it was that he started off just being neighborly to

Jesse. That's what he said, anyway. But clearly they're friends. He also tried to jerk me around and claim he was amazed to hear Jesse dealt drugs. Dom's sure got a smart mouth on him."

"He always did," Carolyn said. "So, you knew about Jesse?"

Art was pretty sure it was just a question and not an accusation. They had reached a tricky intersection, Art realized. But he didn't think he was particularly interested in lying to her. That was a bad start with a woman. With anyone.

"I've had my eye on the situation a little while. But Jesse lives out in the county, on the lake. That's not my turf. And so far as I know he left his business at home when he came to town."

"Did you have hard evidence, Art?"

"No. I did not. Just a whisper or two. His lifestyle. I can put two and two together. But if he had done something in town — out by your high school — he would be behind bars, Carolyn."

"I know that, Art."

"I hope you do. You don't drive off your turf one day and invade someone because of innuendo and such. This isn't Soviet Russia."

He felt that was a little strong, but he wanted to assure her that although he may have been walking a fine line, most of him leaned the right way.

"I'm not faulting you, Art. Not at all. People know you take good care of this town."

He was relieved. "I hope they do. The world's not as black and white as some people think."

"I don't think it is, either."

Art decided that he liked Carolyn very much. "I put you through a ringer today. Sorry. I'll make it up to you."

"Really? How do you top our first date, Art? Burn the town down?" She smiled broadly.

He chuckled. "No more fireworks, I hope. Not ever. I'd be happy to lead a very boring and long life from here on out."

"To a boring but long life," Carolyn said. "More wine, Art?"

"Please. Maybe we should get drunk."

"A little anyway. Excuse me while I go to the little girls' room."

"All the way down the hall, Carolyn."

"I'll find it."

While she was gone he suddenly remembered that Brant Russell's shoulder bag was still in his cruiser. He went outside and got it and when he came back Carolyn had poured him another glass of wine.

"I thought maybe I'd scared you off from your own house, Art."

He sipped his wine and was getting a decent buzz from it. "Thanks. It really hits the spot. No, I just remembered I left this bag out in the car."

"Mr. Russell's bag."

"Yeah. Maybe it tells a story that would be useful to know."

Art unhooked the clasp and looked inside. He was surprised and a little stunned and he took a healthy swig of wine before making eye contact with Carolyn.

"What's in it, Art?"

"Not much," he lied. "Just stuff — like in a lady's purse, really."

"Lipstick and a compact, stuff like that?" she said skeptically.

He tied to grin and act nonchalant at the same time. "That's funny. No, no, it's just stuff. Nothing important. It's just routine evidence to file."

He closed the bag and put the clasp back in place and put the bag on the floor by his feet.

Carolyn squinted a little. "I see. You have an odd look on your face, Art. Are you OK?"

"It must be the wine." He smiled as best as he could. "Yeah, sure, I'm okay. You're right, though. We really should get a little drunk."

Aftermath

39.

Art

After a few weeks Art had resolved everything officially and Dom was even out of the hospital and gingerly back on his feet. No one was charged with anything. As far as Argus knew, Dom and Jesse had tangled unexpectedly with a drug dealer from Indiana passing through town who took offense at a remark and in a struggle his gun went off. It was an accident, which was true to a degree because Dom had meant only to disarm Brant Russell and the gun went off in the struggle. There was a lot more to it than that, but that was where it ended officially. Art had done Jesse and Dom a huge favor and it would soon be time to collect the bill.

Brant Russell had no family. His parents were dead and there was no one else. There had been no parents to receive terrible news and Art was at least happy that was avoided. It was almost as if the man had not existed and in death his disposal became a mere afterthought. He existed for Art, of course, and always would. He knew there would not be a time when what happened wouldn't come to visit him. He felt those visits would be shorter and less frequent as time wore on and he was grateful for that realization and even clung to it a little. But, he realized, he'd finally seen a real war.

The contents of Brant's bag had thrown him for a loop and he had made the decision not to involve Carolyn. It was best she didn't know anything about it. The man's van had a big load of marijuana and speed and confirmed his profession. It had been destroyed, but no one but Art knew about the bag. It contained more than $20,000 in cash. A chunk of change. Art wondered why the man carried so much money, but chalked it up to the mechanics of his trade. And apparently he was pretty good at it. As for disposing of the money, at first Art wasn't sure about where it should go. If Brant Russell had survivors, would it really have gone to them? Art wasn't sure. It was drug money, after all. It wasn't exactly hard-earned honest money. It wasn't the fruits of respectable labor. If he followed proper protocol it would end up with the appropriate authority. He wasn't even sure who that was until he looked into it. The state, perhaps. Or maybe Argus kept it. Something to figure out.

Ideally, Art thought, Brant Russell would have left behind parents who could use the money. It would have helped offset the path he'd chosen in life. Art had been tempted to discuss it with Carolyn. They were getting along very well and becoming close. The shared experience of that day had produced a bond of sorts. And Art had come to see Carolyn as a woman with character and strength. He valued that a lot. But he concluded that she must be kept unaware of it because he had decided on a plan he hoped was defensible and moral and Carolyn must be protected from it.

Morality was a tough subject. Art felt he was a moral man, but he knew it was faulty to believe life was always black and white. That was why he was always so uncomfortable in churches. The gray areas were huge and commonplace. You drove through them like sudden storms.

There were certain official customs to observe. Because Brant Russell had been a drug dealer, it was prudent and expected that money would have been discovered along with the drugs and so in the end Art decided to turn over $5,000 to the proper office and that ended official interest in Brant Russell.

He had to admit that the remaining $15,000 and change was tempting — but not for very long at all. That wasn't how Art saw himself. He didn't covet other people's money. It was important that anything he got he got from his own honest labor. He decided to offer to split the money between Dom and Jesse, to get them started in the right direction. Was that naïve? He hoped not. He didn't think so. Was he trying to play God? No. Instead he believed he was implementing the alternative to what he had chosen not to do: arrest Jesse because he could, and because Jesse qualified for arrest. It seemed to Art that putting Jesse on the right track was a better alternative, one that benefited society — and Jesse — so much more than a costly legal system and jail. He was massaging the rules. He knew that. But people just had to realize that not much should be cast in stone and become immovable.

He even had an out if it ever became necessary: he could always claim he gave them his own money, from the settlement he had gotten from that nearly fatal night in Chicago. That money was invested, growing. He would cash out what he needed and have the bank records to prove it and that would explain it if necessary. He could even turn it all in, claiming the bag was missing for a while. But he didn't think it would come to that. Still, it was prudent, common sense, to be aware of where every road went. There was an element of risk, but Jesse and Dom had a secret to protect, too. Nicole? He couldn't help her directly. But if she and Jesse really were connected and remained so, then she benefited, too. Maybe Jesse would have the good sense to tell Nicole his money was all from his own deals. That would be easy enough to accept. Art didn't want to involve a young lady with a future in such sordid things. Sordid? Too strong. But he didn't want Nicole soiled by it.

That was the plan, anyway. It had all sorts of potential pitfalls, like just about anything in life. It was not a perfect plan and Art knew plenty of people simply would not understand such an arrangement. He could go to jail for it if someone unraveled it sufficiently. He could lose everything he had worked for and the chance for the rest of the things he wanted for himself, but most importantly he could lose his good name and lose himself. He would take the chance, though, in the hope he was right, that life could not always be defined by adhering to man-made conventions and soulless rules. He was betting the farm on his belief that this was one of those gray areas and that helping three people with potential and futures was a better use of the money than just letting it be absorbed by a man-made system without a heart. His only profit would be the satisfaction from helping others. But if it paid off, he felt he would be rich beyond compare.

All that remained was to sell Dom and Jesse. He wasn't out of the woods yet.

40.

Jesse

Jesse was a little surprised — fearful, too — when the Chief asked him to bring Raul by his house for a visit once Raul was getting around pretty good. It had been more than a month since the shooting, but still awfully fresh in his mind. Raul, he saw right away, had adjusted quicker.

"Relax, Jesse. If he was going to arrest you, he would have done it a month ago, man."

"I know. I guess it's just instinct or something. I'm pretty used to always being afraid of cops."

"The Chief ain't a cop," Raul said. "He's a chief of police."

"That's what he likes to say alright."

Jesse pulled the GTO into the Chief's driveway behind the police cruiser.

"Just seeing a cop car gives me the willies," he said.

"Time to break old habits, Jesse. You're a new man. Clean slate, man."

"I reckon so. How about you?"

"Other than this sore shoulder, I'm doing OK."

They had not yet talked about what happened.

"It happened so fast," Jesse said. "Then you were down. Just like that."

"I know," Raul said quietly. "I was there." He rubbed his shoulder.

"Jesus, Raul. I had no fucking idea we'd be talking to Brant one minute and the next the Chief would have to shoot him."

"Mr. Brant made his own bed, Jesse."

"I'm sorry I got you into it. I'm really damn sorry I got you shot, man."

"I got myself into it. Nobody twisted my arm. And the drug lord shot me — not you."

Jesse was getting a little better at accepting it. But it was slow work and some days he still felt awful about it.

Before they reached the Chief's front door, Raul stopped abruptly.

"What's wrong?" Jesse said.

"You're not carrying anything, are you, Jesse?"

Jesse grinned. "No way. Not a thing, man. All gone. Have some faith in me, man."

"Not even a reserve joint, in a pocket?"

"Search me if you want."

"Nothing in the car?"

"Clean as a whistle, Raul."

"Your stash?"

"Up in smoke. Woosh! I made a fire and burned it all."

"All of it?"

"I smoked a last doobie and blared the Stones. No more inventory — it was a fire sale."

They were still laughing when the Chief let them in and led them out to the back porch and got them beers.

"Glad to see you boys in good spirits," the Chief said. "How's that shoulder, Raul?"

"The doctor said some day I'd feel it during winter — arthritis."

"Maybe you need a warm climate," the Chief said.

Raul shook his head. "I already had one — Nam. No more. I reckon I'll stick around here."

"What about you, Jesse?"

"School, I guess, Chief."

"Call me Art, gentlemen. We've all let our slips show one way or another."

"I hear you," Raul said.

Jesse wasn't sure what the Chief meant by it. Something was coming. "For sure — Art."

The Chief excused himself and came back with Brant Russell's canvas bag. Jesse recognized it and his pulse spiked. He looked at Raul, who also looked surprised.

The Chief opened the bag and sat it on the coffee table between them.

"Jesus," Raul said.

"That's quite a loaf of bread you're got there," Jesse said.

"How much?" Raul said.

"Fifteen grand, and some change."

Jesse thought the Chief — Art — looked pretty calm.

"The drug lord was pretty well-heeled," Raul said.

"Who does it go to now?" Jesse said. "Does the town get it?"

"They got theirs already, Jesse. I turned over five grand to them."

"Don't they get it all?" Raul said.

"Do they?" Art said.

"Sonofabitch," Raul said.

"You're keeping it?" Jesse was stunned to think the Chief might be a thief. And why in the fucking world was he telling them?

"No. I've got enough money. I do OK. I've thought about this pretty hard. Lost some sleep over it. I decided I want you two to take it. It's yours, gentlemen. If you want it."

No one spoke for a minute. Jesse wondered if it was somehow an elaborate trap. The three of theme exchanged glances. The Chief fetched three more beers and Jesse and Raul were still twitching a little in their chairs.

"Why?" Jesse finally said.

"Call it an investment."

"In what?" Raul said.

"Your futures, Raul. There's enough to get you guys going somewhere. You served your country, Raul. But what did they leave you with? Thanks and an honorable discharge, that maybe some day you can't even find."

"No one said thanks that I recall," Raul said.

"There you go," Art said.

"I didn't serve my country," Jesse said.

"Doesn't matter," Art said. "Maybe you need it the most, Jesse."

"I saved a few bucks."

"Now you have some more. School isn't cheap."

"Would it be right?" Jesse said.

"Is putting money to its best use the right thing to do, Jesse?"

"There's rules," Raul said.

"And we need them," Art said. "But sometimes rules don't do a good enough job of putting things right. Sometimes they fall short. That's when people have to act. The town didn't earn this money. It's money that fell out of the sky. And they got five grand anyway. Maybe they buy a new snowplow. One day the mayor will remind me I did a great job and point at the shiny new snowplow."

"Nobody earned this money," Jesse said. "It doesn't even exist."

"I disagree," Art said. "All three of us paid a price. Because of it, I believe you two have earned it."

"What about your share?" Raul said.

"I can't," Art said. "I've already pushed the law as far as it can be pushed. I can't and still be a cop. And I choose to remain a cop, so that's that."

"What if we tell someone where we got it?" Raul said.

Art shrugged. "I cashed out a mutual fund from my bank. I can always say I gave it to you two to help a returned vet and promising college student. People would call me a hero — again. All the ministers in town would mention me in their sermons. Word would get out that Jesse dealt drugs. You might even be branded a vindictive, confused vet pissed about getting shot. The town would have its snowplow. Who will people believe?"

"Far out," Jesse said.

Art walked them out to the car.

"What if we just blow it?" Raul said.

"Up to you," Art said. "I did my part. I'll take the risk."

41.

Raul

They cruised slowly down Main Street after dividing the money. Raul got rid of the canvas bag in a dumpster at Gilstrap's Texaco.

"That's the last of Brant Russell," Raul said when he tossed the bag.

"But not his money."

"I guess the man had a purpose after all, Jesse."

"Where do you want to go, Raul? You want to come out to the lake? Maybe get something to eat?"

Raul thought about it for a few blocks. "No, just drop me at the VFW."

"Really? I thought you didn't like that place?"

"It's OK, I guess. If I go home, my folks will just try to smother me. There's plenty of time for that shit."

Jesse pulled over and parked in front of the VFW.

"You going home, Jesse?"

"Home. Where's home, Raul?"

"The lake. Summer's practically here, dude. You said something about fishing."

"We could do that."

"Sure we could, Jesse."

"It's a nice thought. But I'm done with the lake. It would just remind me of things."

"I know. Where will you go?"

"Today, over to Bloomington. I guess I should find out what it takes to go back to school. Then Ferguson's, to see Nicole."

"Sounds like a plan, Jesse. Where's that Nicole thing going?"

"Maybe nowhere. Maybe everywhere. Too soon to tell."

"But worth the ride."

"Absolutely."

Raul got out, but leaned back in the passenger window.

"We did the right thing, Jesse. The money, I mean."

"I feel selfish. A little anyway."

"Me, too. But guess what, that means it's OK to use it. If we didn't feel that way, we wouldn't deserve it."

"That's probably what the Chief would say — Art."

"He would. He absolutely would. Are you going to tell Nicole?"

"No. She knows I saved some bread. That will just have to explain it."

"Cool," Raul said. "OK, man. You take care."

"I will. Don't tell too many tall tales in there."

"A couple small ones maybe."

They shook hands through the window, then Jesse pulled out and Raul watched the GTO until it was out of sight. He went inside the VFW and sat at the bar and the bartender nodded and pushed a coaster toward him. A couple men he knew to be World War II vets acknowledged him from stools a few yards down the bar.

"What'll you drink?" the bartender said.

"Whatever's cold."

Raul took his beer and sat with the two other vets and after a while he had to remind himself about all the money in his pockets.

42.

Jesse

He left the ISU campus with a new college catalogue and fresh dreams. A counselor had encouraged his interest in the journalism program and gave him a breakdown of the classes he'd need. It was three years of work, but he finally felt it was something he could do. He could learn. He was sure of it. Well, fairly sure. He didn't know if he really could become a writer, but he wanted to try. Jesse drove around campus and tried to recover the feelings he'd once had as a college student. Who he was before he hopped on the dope train and rode it too far. Jesse looked at the faces of the few students he saw and they all seemed fresh, and even hopeful. He glanced at his own face in the mirror and had to laugh because he felt he looked more confused than hopeful.

Jesse stopped at a pizza place he'd frequented when he'd first gone to ISU. Inside, it was exactly as it had been during his time a few years before: smoky, poorly lit, and picnic tables with thousands of initials carved in them. Those worn and mutilated tables were sort of the place's trademark. They made good pizza, served pissy beer — Budweiser, Busch, Old Style — and the aroma of baking dough and sausage and pepperoni filled the place. A few students sat at the small bar and drank Budweiser in mugs and paid no mind to Jesse as he stood near the bar and surveyed the room. He took a stool at the end near the door with his back toward it. After a minute he realized he would have never done that the past couple years. When he was a dealer he always sat where he could watch the door and everyone who came through it. Now he didn't care.

Jesse drank a mug of Busch and listened to a couple students who came in and sat down just a couple stools away. They were talking about summer school classes and were very excited about it. One of them bragged that he could graduate in just three years if he kept up his pace. The other doubted it and predicted his friend would hit a wall academically and mentally and be forced to cut back. But to Jesse it seemed clear that they had an aura of success about them fueled by determination. He wondered how he'd managed to lose that a few years before. It just happened, he concluded. One day the air just goes all out of something. There wasn't always an answer to things. They just stop one day without an earth-shattering reason. But you could get it back. Listening to those two students actually looking forward to the hard work and long hours made him realize he could definitely get it fucking back. You just had to want it and then move your ass in the right direction. He bought the two students a round.

"Thanks, man," the three-year plan man said. The other nodded, raised his mug in salute.

"Happy birthday," Jesse said, raising his mug, too.

The two students looked confused, but smiled.

"It's not my birthday," the three-year man said.

The other shrugged. "Me, neither."

"I was just saying that," Jesse said. "I'm feeling good."

"Here's to feeling good," the three-year man said. "What's the occasion?"

Jesse mulled it a few seconds and gulped some beer.

"I dodged a bullet."

"You did?"

"I sure as shit did," Jesse said, gulping more beer.

"What kind of bullet?" the three-year man said.

"A pretty big one," Jesse said.

"Close, was it?" the three-year man said.

"Yeah," Jesse said. "It was. But you know, a miss is as good as a mile."

Jesse finished his beer and bought another round for the two students and left. He drove back to his trailer with a sense of purpose he hadn't had in years. If he really wasn't a dealer anymore, as he kept telling himself at the bar, then there was just the one more thing to do. Action, not words. It was too warm for a fire, but he built one anyway and retrieved his stash and burned it. He had pounds of marijuana and bags of speed and a few bricks of hash. It was worth a chunk of change but he no longer cared and even laughed, reminding himself that not so long ago at all the thought of torching it would have been unthinkable. Now it was easy and he dumped it all on the consuming fire and it made a strong odor and the flames flickered orange and blue and yellow and red and he watched the smoke plume billow up above the trees and he felt that part of his life drift away with the smoke.

Satisfied, he drove the GTO very fast to Argus, but halfway there he abruptly pulled over. A wave of doubt washed over him and he felt an odd chill despite the warm air. Could he trust what Nicole was? What was she exactly? His girlfriend, he reckoned. Was that right? She was awfully structured, organized — opinionated. Did that really fit with him? He wasn't sure why Nicole liked him. Did she? How dumb. Why would she bother with him if she didn't?

He got out and walked around the GTO and looked off across the cornfields. The corn would grow tall very soon until no one could see over it. Jesse instinctively rummaged through his pockets for a joint that wasn't there and concluded he was glad it wasn't.

Jesse drove in to Argus and went to Ferguson's. Nicole was checking groceries and he stood a moment watching her, trying to understand who she was. It was a mystery and he wanted to solve it but wasn't sure where to begin. Attraction was an odd thing. It made no sense, really. It was all chemicals and emotions and — blind, dumb luck, perhaps. One day the air goes out, and one day the air goes back in. One day you're alone, and the next you have the responsibility of someone else, and the challenge of making sense of it. And there is no road map, no owner's manual — you just flopped around like fish on a dock and hoped you made it into the safety of the water.

Nicole looked up and saw him, and for a moment, he thought — was it his imagination? — she seemed not to recognize him. It was a brief moment, but heavy with dullness, he thought. Then she smiled and when her last customer was gone he went over and explained his new plans.

"That's great, Jesse. It really is."

"I'm ready," he said. "I can do it. I know I can."

"So do I. I'm proud of you."

"Are you really?"

"Of course. It's a big step. I think you can do anything you put your mind to."

Jesse kissed Nicole right there at her register amid a smiling audience of housewives and left her actually blushing. Outside he looked in the window and waved, but she was already back to checking groceries. He pulled out of the Ferguson's lot and rolled down Main Street toward the lake. The possibilities seemed unlimited. At the last stoplight Art pulled alongside him in the next lane.

"Hell of a day for a drive," Art said.

Jesse smiled back. "Especially out at the lake, Chief." He thought of his stash going up in flames and the smoke cloud and wondered what the Chief would think of it.

"Art, Jesse. Just call me Art."

"Right. Art."

"Where you headed, Jesse?"

"On down the road."

"Going far?"

"I aim to."

"I suspect that's so."

Art saluted and pulled ahead through the green light. Jesse hesitated a moment, then followed him until Art turned off at his street and then Jesse gunned the GTO and sped toward the lake feeling as light as a feather.

43.

Nicole

She already had some doubts about Jesse, but chalked it all up to the normal give and take of a new relationship. Perhaps some of it was also the natural fallout of being just a little bit stunned — rather horrified, at first, was accurate — by the shooting and Jesse's involvement. But she was satisfied, mostly, that it was just bad luck — being in the wrong place at the wrong time — and that Jesse was on the path to reform and stability. He said all the right things, anyway, and exuded the proper amount of enthusiasm and excitement, and so she was willing to let it ride. There were always bumps in the road and she accepted that.

On her next day off she drove to ISU and registered for fall. The plan was for her and Jesse to get a place together. It was all fairly romantic, if not luxurious. There would be dues to pay. She could work nights at the IGA grocery store in Bloomington. There were very cheap apartments on the edge of campus and Jesse had already checked them out. She drove by them, too, the day she registered and thought they seemed acceptable. Dull and gray, but that was just the outside.

But what did they really need to go to school? Some furniture, a good and solid table for meals, and a comfortable bed. Jesse was taking care of all that. That pleased her a lot. He seemed to have accumulated a lot of money from dealing and now they would spend some of it to get going. He would find a part-time job, too, and they would have to pinch a few pennies when the drug money ran out, but she felt they could handle it. Nice things would come later. You worked for those things, she reminded herself, and if you had to sacrifice a while at first and go without, it would just make you appreciate all the more what you earned.

Little things could be done to make an apartment a home and she was already thinking of what candles and incense and posters could do to spice up a place with a few splashes of color here and there. Curtains were essential. Good curtains could make a room and she already had some ideas and was eager to see one of the apartments. Jesse had a good stereo and they would live in a world of good music and make friends quickly and have them over to groove to the tunes and eat dinners they all contributed to make.

And they would learn. Jesse would learn to be a writer and she would explore the world of psychology. She wanted to learn. She felt she knew much already, about people, about how life worked. But she wanted more and hungered for it so much that she went to the campus bookstore and bought a book on psychology and sat on a bench outside to read. When students walked by she looked up and smiled and felt, as she was sure they certainly must have felt also, that they were all members of the same tribe.

1975

44.

Art

He finished the day's reports and decided to drive the town. Art always looked forward to getting out among the people and seeing what the town was up to. It was the best part of the job. The rain had finally stopped and the sun was slowly burning through the receding gray clouds. It had been a wet and soggy spring that lasted well into May before people were willing to concede there really would be a summer. He walked across the street to Cameron's and got a coffee to-go and chatted a few minutes with a gaggle of farmers who were happy about the rain.

He drove one of the side streets east toward the outskirts of town, out by the grain elevator and fields of sprouting corn and soybeans. There was a new subdivision there, one of large and ambitious homes with only saplings trucked in to pass off as trees. The houses seemed out of place to Art, as though they were tall-masted ships that had run aground. Argus had grown noticeably the past five years and the subdivision was inching ever closer toward the Sangamon River.

Art did not know these new people very well yet. Most of them worked for State Farm in Bloomington, or at ISU. They had been attracted by the wide-open spaces and the illusion they could become country squires; but Art had no quarrel with that, really. To each his own. He would get to know the ones who frequented Cameron's, or who stopped in Bunnie's Tavern for an after-work drink. Bunnie's had responded to the white-collar growth and expanded its menu to include wine and martinis. He would likely know almost nothing about the ones who largely bypassed Argus except to buy groceries or plumbing supplies on weekends at Fleener's Hardware — unless they had trouble, and then of course Art would become their new best friend. That was the worst of the job, but a part he accepted as the toll to travel the road.

There were short streets barely connected to the town he had not driven in a while and he drove them slowly, reacquainting himself with those neighborhoods, waving at a few children playing, mothers chatting on sidewalks. A dog ran alongside his cruiser for a block, barking noisily before finally giving up. Art chuckled as he looked in his rearview mirror at the dog still standing defiantly in the middle of the street. He cruised those tucked-away streets until he felt he knew them as well as any others.

Art drove back to Main Street and cruised it slowly, watching people skirt puddles of water, some still with open umbrellas, as they crossed the street. He passed the VFW and saw Mayor Sullivan about to enter. The mayor looked up from his mild alcohol stupor and waved enthusiastically. Art countered with a salute. Down the block on the other side of the street he passed Ferguson's IGA, where Nicole had checked his groceries years before, and that suddenly made him think of Jesse and Dominick, and the deal they had made.

Had it really been five years? Some days it seemed like just yesterday, or the day before that. Sometimes it seemed like a decade. On the days when it seemed to have just happened, his memory of it was clear and events played out in his head in slow-motion, an agonizingly slow-motion, with brilliant colors and the sharp bangs — each bullet fired distinct and not run together with the others. But when those days, those memories, seemed remote and something instead out of a dusty history book, what had happened was jumbled and out-of-focus, vague — dark and silent, almost — and gave him the sense that it had not really happened at all.

On this day, the memories were somewhere in the middle of those two dream worlds: distant and cloudy on the one hand, but still in sharp enough clarity to make him feel the old chill of it for a moment before accepting the memory and not buying into the regret. But it forced him to pull over to the curb a moment to let the ghosts slowly dissipate. There he sat and watched people on the sidewalks. Many waved to him and he managed a clumsy smile and waved back.

As he sat, he forced himself out of the past, with some effort, and chose to get past it the way people sometimes forced themselves not to glance at a cemetery despite the headstones in their peripheral vision. He saw the prime players, clearly, one at a time: Dom had drifted for nearly a year after being shot and mostly showed up at the VFW, where he felt most comfortable with other veterans. Art had looked in on him from time to time and finally decided that Dom had needed more time to tell his own story of war to the other veterans, and in the process finally shed enough of Vietnam to begin thinking about other things. Finally Dom made his way to the community college over in Champaign and studied drafting and got a job in Colorado, where the mountains and snow were so different from Vietnam that he finally felt at home, and at peace. He had come home the previous year to visit his folks and bought Art a beer at the VFW. The deal they had made never came up, nor would it.

Jesse and Nicole moved in together in Bloomington and Jesse got his degree in journalism and a reporting job with the Pantagraph. He had the ability after all to craft good and clear sentences and to tell a story with them. But after a couple years, Jesse and Nicole apparently woke up one morning and realized they were becoming strangers drifting in different directions. Nicole finished school in Champaign, at the University of Illinois, and did finally become a social worker in Chicago as she worked on becoming a psychologist. Good for her, Art thought happily. She was a very smart and tough girl and deserved to get what she wanted, what she needed. Nicole married an accountant who met her standards of ambition and they bought a nice home in Oak Park.

Jesse left for a paper in Arizona, figuring that the longer he stayed in central Illinois, the more likely it was he might run into former drug customers. And he had developed the urge to see more of the world. Art attended a police chiefs' convention in Tucson and had lunch with Jesse, who had sold the GTO, cut his hair short and even wore ties to work. They laughed about Jesse's latest story, which was an assessment of drug activity in Arizona. Jesse had a Hispanic girlfriend, a copy editor at his paper, and it seemed to Art that marriage might be in the cards for them. That gave Art a very satisfying feeling. He had invested in Jesse — more than just the money. If some people knew the room he had given Jesse at the beginning, would they understand? It didn't matter. His gamble had paid off and he knew he had done the right thing. That was his take in the deal. That meant more to him than any amount of cash from the deal could have provided.

As for Brant Russell, Art had made the best peace treaty he could with that ghost. The man visited him from time to time and Art endured it and tried to pretend it was no worse than unwelcome and tiresome relatives come to roost for a weekend. It was not that simple, of course, nor easy, but Art had noticed the visits did seem shorter and less frequent over time and he accepted it as the terrible price of ending a life, no matter how justified. He prayed for the soul of Brant Russell sometimes, in his own private way — without the confines of a church. He also prayed for Dom, Jesse, and Nicole, but felt they would all be just fine. Several ministers had invited him to their churches to worship, to cleanse him, he supposed, of his ordeal — his sins. He did not think he had sinned and politely appeared at each church and then just as politely excused himself at the first opportunity and left.

Satisfied with the disposition of his town, Art drove on out of Argus and turned down the road to the lake — the road home. The year before he had finally made the move and bought a nice home with a good view of the water. It was his dream house, the one he always felt was there for him with just hard work and a desire to keep that dream alive. He had his little boat dock and a small boat with an Evinrude outboard for puttering about in a cove protected from the wind. On this day, the sun had finally asserted itself and cast the clouds aside and Art pulled into his drive and got out to a beautiful sunset. He slipped off his shoes and socks and felt the wet grass beneath his feet. The lake was calm and glassy and a few sailboats had appeared, red and yellow dots at the far end of the lake working their way toward him.

He strolled down to his dock and leaned on the railing and smelled the freshness of the lake. Ducks rounded a nearby point, in line and chattering noisily, happily. After a while, Art heard footsteps on the wooden planks behind him, the best sound he had heard for a long time, and he turned and smiled at Carolyn, who handed him a martini and took her place at the railing.

Michael Loyd Gray

Michael Loyd Gray was born in Jonesboro, Arkansas, in the shadow of Graceland and Elvis Presley, the land of RC Colas and Moon Pies, but grew up in Champaign, IL.

Gray graduated from the University of Illinois with a Journalism degree and was a newspaper staff writer in Arizona and Illinois for ten years, conducting the last interview of novelist Erskine Caldwell. He earned an MFA in English from Western Michigan University and has taught at colleges and universities in upstate New York, Michigan, Illinois, Wisconsin, and Texas.

He is the winner of the 2005 Alligator Juniper Fiction Prize, the 2005 The Writers Place Award for Fiction. His novel *Not Famous Anymore* was awarded a grant by the Elizabeth George Foundation, and his novel *December's Children* was a finalist for Sol Books Prose Series Prize.

He now lives in Kalamazoo, MI, with two insolent cats, EH and Moonpie.

SOL Books Poetry Series

Pacific
by Scott R. Welvaert
ISBN 978-0-9793081-0-9

Two star-crossed lovers, David and Marti,
set out to fulfill their dying wish: see the
Pacific Ocean. They begin in Minnesota,
where they meet at an AIDS clinic, and
Pacific chronicles David and Marti's journey
through the Black Hills, past Devil's Tower,
and to Cannon Beach. Before reaching
their destination, they must first accept
their fates and the past choices that have led
them down this tragic road.

SOL Books Prose Series

The Prostitutes of Post Office Street
by Frank F. Carden
ISBN 978-0-9793081-2-3

Post Office Street drops readers into the
red-light district of Galveston, where
crooked cops and down-on-their-luck
prostitutes dwell. Yet, in this seedy
part of town, Carden paints a picture
of hope as his characters seek to rise
above the pain of broken hearts and
misplaced passions.

SOL Books Upper Midwest Writers Series

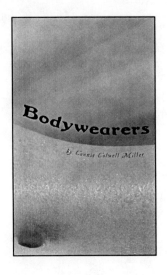

Bodywearers
by Connie Colwell Miller
ISBN 978-0-9793081-1-6

Whether Miller writes of a red-tailed hawk hunting for mice or a lover's underwear crumpled up on the bedroom floor, her voice is filled with a revealing breath of candor, drawing our attention to the small details in nature and of the body, often showing us beauty where we may not have expected it..

My Father's Gloves
by David Speiring
ISBN 978-0-9793081-6-1

My Father's Gloves touches on that most-conflicted of family bonds, the one between fathers and sons. With a hauntingly painful voice, Spiering explores the burdensome yoke of a father's expectations and the struggles a son must face as he grows into manhood.

LaVergne, TN USA
19 November 2010

205555LV00001B/5/P